A LANDSCAPE PAINTER

A LANDSCAPE PAINTER

By

HENRY JAMES

Short Story Index Reprint Series

BOOKS FOR LIBRARIES PRESS
FREEPORT, NEW YORK

First Published 1919
Reprinted 1970

INTERNATIONAL STANDARD BOOK NUMBER:
0-8369-3749-X

LIBRARY OF CONGRESS CATALOG·CARD NUMBER:
70-142265

PRINTED IN THE UNITED STATES OF AMERICA

CONTENTS

PREFACE
(TO ORIGINAL EDITION)

THE four tales comprising this volume are printed now for the first time in America in book form. All of them were written by Henry James before he had attained his twenty-fifth year. They are remarkable for their maturity of thought and clarity of style.

It has been the general opinion that James, like George Eliot, achieved his literary development rather slowly, since it was known that he was thirty-two years of age when "The Passionate Pilgrim," his first collection of tales, and "Rodrick Hudson," his first long novel, were published. As a matter of fact, however, James had been writing for the leading magazines since he was twenty-two. The first story in this volume, "A Landscape Painter," appeared in the *Atlantic Monthly* for February, 1866, and was the second story James had published up to that time.

The tales in this volume are among the most precious in our literature, and James himself thought

1

highly of them, since he collected them in an English edition, published in 1885, in three volumes with the title, "Short Stories Revived." This collection never appeared in America. It is strange that James should have chosen to appeal to English readers rather than to his own countrymen. Why he did so is a question that remains unanswered. But the present volume will serve as a corrective of this anomaly. The tales are reprinted, not from the English edition, but from the American periodicals in which they were first published.

It has been claimed for William Dean Howells that it was he who discovered James, when, as assistant editor to Fields on the *Atlantic Monthly,* he strongly recommended the acceptance of James' story, "Poor Richard." The claim, however, is not altogether well founded, since James had published two stories before that time. These were "A Landscape Painter" and "A Day of Days," the latter appearing in the *Galaxy* for June 15, 1866. All three stories are reprinted in this volume.

Unusual interest, however, attaches to the tale of "Poor Richard," because of Howell's connection with it. Its reading led to the beginning of a friendship between James and Howells which may be considered as one of the great literary friendships in the annals of literature. Howells told the story in the *Century* for November, 1882.

When the manuscript was received at the office of the *Atlantic,* Fields submitted it to Howells for his opinion. Howells read it, and when asked whether he would accept it, he replied, "Yes, and all the stories you can get from that writer." "One is much securer of one's judgment," writes Howells, "at twenty-nine than, say, at forty-five; but if there was a mistake, I am not yet old enough to regret it. The story was called 'Poor Richard' and it dealt with the conscience of a man very much in love with a woman who loved his rival. He told the rival a lie, which sent him away to his death on the field, but poor Richard's lie did not win his love. It seems to me that the situation was strongly and finely felt. One's pity went, as it should, with the liar; but the whole story has a pathos which lingers in my mind equally with a sense of the new literary qualities which gave me much delight in it."

The final story of this volume, "A Most Extraordinary Case," was first published in the *Atlantic Monthly* for April, 1868, when Howells was still on the editorial staff.

I am sure these first efforts of James' pen will be welcomed by his American admirers. They are in every way worthy of James at his best. Far from detracting from his reputation, many a reader will no doubt feel regret that the author should in his later works have seen fit to adopt an elaborate, complex and often obscure style, instead of clinging to simple, natural language, of which these stories show him to be such a master.

ALBERT MORDELL.

Philadelphia, July 10, 1919.

A LANDSCAPE PAINTER

A LANDSCAPE
PAINTER

D O you remember how, a dozen years ago,
a number of our friends were startled by
the report of the rupture of young Locksley's engagement with Miss Leary? This event
made some noise in its day. Both parties possessed
certain claims to distinction: Locksley in his wealth,
which was believed to be enormous, and the young
lady in her beauty, which was in truth very great.
I used to hear that her lover was fond of compar-
ing her to the Venus of Milo; and, indeed, if you
can imagine the mutilated goddess with her full
complement of limbs, dressed out by Madame de
Crinoline, and engaged in small talk beneath the
drawing-room chandelier, you may obtain a vague
notion of Miss Josephine Leary. Locksley, you remember, was rather a short man, dark, and not
particularly good-looking; and when he walked
about with his betrothed, it was half a matter of

7

surprise that he should have ventured to propose to
a young lady of such heroic proportions. Miss
Leary had the gray eyes and auburn hair which I
have always assigned to the famous statue. The
one defect in her face, in spite of an expression of
great candor and sweetness, was a certain lack of
animation. What it was besides her beauty that
attracted Locksley I never discovered: perhaps,
since his attachment was so short-lived, it was her
beauty alone. I say that his attachment was of
brief duration, because the rupture was understood
to have come from him. Both he and Miss Leary
very wisely held their tongues on the matter; but
among their friends and enemies it of course received a hundred explanations. That most popular
with Locksley's well-wishers was that he had backed
out (these events are discussed, you know, in fash-
ionable circles very much as an expected prize-
fight which has miscarried is canvassed in reunions
of another kind) only on flagrant evidence of the
lady's — what, faithlessness? — on overwhelming
proof of the most *mercenary* spirit on the part of
Miss Leary. You see, our friend was held capable
of doing battle for an "idea." It must be owned
that this was a novel charge; but, for myself, having long known Mrs. Leary, the mother, who was a

widow with four daughters, to be an inveterate old screw, I took the liberty of accrediting the existence of a similar propensity in her eldest born. I suppose that the young lady's family had, on their own side, a very plausible version of their disappointment. It was, however, soon made up to them by Josephine's marriage with a gentleman of expectations very nearly as brilliant as those of her old suitor. And what was *his* compensation? That is precisely my story.

Locksley disappeared, as you will remember, from public view. The events above alluded to happened in March. On calling at his lodgings in April, I was told he had gone to the "country." But towards the last of May I met him. He told me that he was on the look-out for a quiet, unfrequented place on the seashore, where he might rusticate and sketch. He was looking very poorly. I suggested Newport, and I remember he hardly had the energy to smile at the simple joke. We parted without my having been able to satisfy him, and for a very long time I quite lost sight of him. He died seven years ago, at the age of thirty-five. For five years, accordingly, he managed to shield his life from the eyes of men. Through circumstances which I need not detail, a large portion of his personal property has

come into my hands. You will remember that he
was a man of what are called elegant tastes: that
is, he was seriously interested in arts and letters.
He wrote some very bad poetry, but he produced
a number of remarkable paintings. He left a mass
of papers on all subjects, few of which are adapted
to be generally interesting. A portion of them, however, I highly prize,—that which constitutes his
private diary. It extends from his twenty-fifth to
his thirtieth year, at which period it breaks off
suddenly. If you will come to my house, I will
show you such of his pictures and sketches as I
possess, and, I trust, convert you to my opinion that
he had in him the stuff of a great painter. Meanwhile I will place before you the last hundred pages
of his diary, as an answer to your inquiry regarding the ultimate view taken by the great Nemesis
of his treatment of Miss Leary,—his scorn of the
magnificent Venus Victrix. The recent decease of
the one person who had a voice paramount to mine
in the disposal of Locksley's effects enables me to
act without reserve.

Cragthrope, June 9th.—I have been sitting some
minutes, pen in hand, pondering whether on this
new earth, beneath this new sky, I had better resume
these occasional records of my idleness. I think

I will at all events make the experiment. If we fail,
as Lady Macbeth remarks, we fail. I find my en-
tries have been longest when my life has been dull-
est. I doubt not, therefore, that, once launched
into the monotony of village life, I shall sit scrib-
bling from morning till night. If nothing hap-
pens—— But my prophetic soul tells me that
something *will* happen. I am determined that something shall,—if it be nothing else than that I paint
a picture.

When I came up to bed half an hour ago, I was
deadly sleepy. Now, after looking out of the window a little while, my brain is strong and clear, and
I feel as if I could write till morning. But, unfortunately, I have nothing to write about. And then,
if I expect to rise early, I must turn in betimes. The
whole village is asleep, godless metropolitan that I
am! The lamps on the square without flicker in the
wind; there is nothing abroad but the blue darkness
and the smell of the rising tide. I have spent the
whole day on my legs, trudging from one side of
the peninsula to the other. What a trump is old
Mrs. M——, to have thought of this place! I must
write her a letter of passionate thanks. Never before, it seems to me, have I known pure coast-scen-
ery. Never before have I relished the beauties of
wave, rock, and cloud. I am filled with a sensuous
ecstasy at the unparalleled life, light, and trans-

parency of the air. I am stricken mute with reverent admiration at the stupendous resources possessed by the ocean in the way of color and sound; and as yet, I suppose, I have not seen half of them. I came in to supper hungry, weary, footsore, sunburnt, dirty,—happier, in short, than I have been for a twelvemonth. And now for the victories of the brush!

June 11th.—Another day afoot and also afloat. I resolved this morning to leave this abominable little tavern. I can't stand my feather-bed another night. I determined to find some other prospect than the town-pump and the "drug-store." I questioned my host, after breakfast, as to the possibility of getting lodgings in any of the outlying farms and cottages. But my host either did not or would not know anything about the matter. So I resolved to wander forth and seek my fortune,—to roam inquisitive through the neighborhood, and appeal to the indigenous sentiment of hospitality. But never did I see a folk so devoid of this amiable quality. By dinner-time I had given up in despair. After dinner I strolled down to the harbor, which is close at hand. The brightness and breeziness of the water tempted me to hire a boat and resume my explorations. I procured an old tub, with a short stump of a mast, which, being planted quite in the centre, gave the craft much the appearance of an inverted mushroom. I made for what I took to be, and what is, an island, lying long and low, some three or four miles, over against the town. I sailed for half an hour directly before the wind, and at last found myself aground on the shelving beach of a quiet little cove. *Such* a little cove! So bright, so still, so warm, so remote from the town, which lay off in the distance, white and semicircular! I leaped ashore, and dropped my anchor. Before me rose a steep cliff, crowned with an old ruined fort or tower. I made my way up, and about to the landward entrance. The fort is a hollow old shell. Looking upward from the beach, you see the harmless blue sky through the gaping loopholes. Its interior is choked with rocks and brambles, and masses of fallen masonry. I scrambled up to the parapet, and obtained a noble sea-view. Beyond the broad bay I saw miniature town and country mapped out before me; and on the other hand, I saw the infinite Atlantic,—over which, by the by, all the pretty things are brought from Paris. I spent the whole afternoon in wandering hither and thither over the hills that encircle the little cove in which I had landed, heedless of the minutes and my steps, watching the sailing clouds and the cloudy sails on the horizon, listening to the musical attrition of the tidal pebbles, killing innocuous suckers. The only particular sensation I remember was that of being ten years old again, together with a general impression of Saturday afternoon, of the liberty to go in wading or even swimming, and of the prospect of limping home in the dusk with a wondrous story of having *almost* caught a turtle. When I returned, I found—but I know very well what I found, and I need hardly repeat it here for my mortification. Heaven knows I never was a practical character. What thought I about the tide? There lay the old tub, high and dry, with the rusty anchor protruding from the flat green stones and the shallow puddles left by the receding wave. Moving the boat an inch, much more a dozen yards, was quite beyond my strength. I slowly reascended the cliff, to see if from its summit any help was discernible. None was within sight; and I was about to go down again in profound dejection, when I saw a trim little sailboat shoot out from behind a neighboring bluff, and advance along the shore. I quickened pace. On reaching the beach, I found the newcomer standing out about a hundred yards. The man at the helm appeared to regard me with some interest. With a mute prayer that his feeling might be akin to compassion, I invited him by voice and gesture to make for a little point of rocks a short distance above us, where I proceeded to join him. I told him my story, and he readily took me aboard. He was a civil old gentleman, of the seafaring sort, who appeared to be cruising about in the evening breeze for his pleasure. On landing, I visited the proprietor of my old tub, related my misadventure, and offered to pay damages, if the boat should turn out in the morning to have sustained any. Meanwhile, I suppose, it is held secure against the next tidal revolution, however insidious.—But for my old gentleman. I have decidedly picked up an acquaintance, if not made a friend. I gave him a very good cigar; and before we reached home, we had become thoroughly intimate. In exchange for my cigar, he gave me his name; and there was that in his tone which seemed to imply that I had by no means the worst of the bargain. His name is Richard Blunt, "though most people," he added, "call me Captain, for short." He then proceeded to inquire my own titles and pretensions. I told him no lies, but I told him only half the truth; and if he chooses to indulge mentally in any romantic understatements, why, he is welcome, and bless his simple heart! The fact is, that I have broken with the past. I have decided, coolly and calmly, as I believe, that it is necessary to my success, or, at any rate, to my happiness, to abjure for a while my conventional self, and to assume a simple, natural character. How can a man be simple and natural who is known to have a hundred thousand a year? That is the supreme curse. It's bad enough to have it: to be known to have it, to be known only because you have it, is most damnable. I suppose I am too proud to be successfully rich. Let me see how poverty will serve my turn. I have taken a fresh start. I have determined to stand upon my own merits. If they fail me, I shall fall back upon my millions; but with God's help I will test them, and see what kind of stuff I am made of. To be young, to be strong, to be poor,—such, in this blessed nineteenth century, is the great basis of solid success. I have resolved to take at least one brief draught from the pure founts of inspiration of my time. I replied to the Captain with such reservations as a brief survey of these principles dictated. What a luxury to pass in a poor man's mind for his brother! I begin to respect myself. Thus much the Captain knows: that I am an educated man, with a taste for painting; that I have come hither for the purpose of cultivating this taste by the study of coast scenery, and for my health. I have reason to believe, moreover, that he suspects me of limited means and of being a good deal of an economist. Amen! *Vogue la galère!* But the point of my story is in his very hospitable offer of lodgings. I had been telling him of my ill success of the morning in the pursuit of the same. He is an odd union of the gentleman of the old school and the old-fashioned, hot-headed merchant-captain. I suppose that certain traits in these characters are readily convertible.

"Young man," said he, after taking several meditative puffs of his cigar, "I don't see the point of your living in a tavern, when there are folks about you with more house-room than they know what to do with. A tavern is only half a house, just as one of these new-fashioned screw-propellers is only half a ship. Suppose you walk round and take a look at my place. I own quite a respectable house over yonder to the left of the town. Do you see that old wharf with the tumble-down warehouses, and the long row of elms behind it? I live right in the midst of the elms. We have the dearest little garden in the world, stretching down to the water's edge. It's all as quiet as anything can be, short of a graveyard. The back windows, you know, overlook the harbor; and you can see twenty miles up the bay, and fifty miles out to sea. You can paint to yourself there the livelong day, with no more fear of intrusion than if you were out yonder at the light-ship. There's no one but myself and my daughter, who's a perfect lady, Sir. She teaches music in a young ladies' school. You see, money's an object, as they say. We have never taken boarders yet, because none came in our track; but I guess we can learn the ways. I suppose you've boarded before; you can put us up to a thing or two."

There was something so kindly and honest in the old man's weather-beaten face, something so friendly in his address, that I forthwith struck a bargain with him, subject to his daughter's approval. I am to have her answer to-morrow. This same daughter strikes me as rather a dark spot in the picture. Teacher in a young ladies' school,—probably the establishment of which Mrs. M—— spoke to me. I suppose she's over thirty. I think I know the species.

June 12th, A.M.—I have really nothing to do but to scribble. "Barkis is willing." Captain Blunt brought me word this morning that his daughter smiles propitious. I am to report this evening; but I shall send my slender baggage in an hour or two.

P. M.—Here I am, housed. The house is less than a mile from the inn, and reached by a very pleasant road, skirting the harbor. At about six o'clock I presented myself. Captain Blunt had described the place. A very civil old negress admitted me, and ushered me into the garden, where I found my friends watering their flowers. The old man was in his house-coat and slippers. He gave me a cordial welcome. There is something delightfully easy in his manners,—and in Miss Blunt's, too, for that matter. She received me very nicely. The late Mrs. Blunt was probably a well-bred woman.

As for Miss Blunt's being thirty, she is about twenty-four. She wore a fresh white dress, with a violet ribbon at her neck, and a rosebud in her button-hole,—or whatever corresponds thereto on the feminine bosom. I thought I discerned in this costume a vague intention of courtesy, of deference, of celebrating my arrival. I don't believe Miss Blunt wears white muslin every day. She shook hands with me, and made me a very frank little speech about her hospitality. "We have never had any inmates before," said she; "and we are, consequently, new to the business. I don't know what you expect. I hope you don't expect a great deal. You must ask for anything you want. If we can give it, we shall be very glad to do so; if we can't, I give you warning that we shall refuse outright." Bravo, Miss Blunt! The best of it is, that she is decidedly beautiful,—and in the grand manner: tall, and rather plump. What is the orthodox description of a pretty girl?—white and red? Miss Blunt is not a pretty girl, she is a handsome woman. She leaves an impression of black and red; that is, she is a florid brunette. She has a great deal of wavy black hair, which encircles her head like a dusky glory, a smoky halo. Her eyebrows, too, are black, but her eyes themselves are of a rich blue gray, the color of those slate-cliffs which I saw yesterday, weltering under the tide. Her mouth, however, is her strong

point. It is very large, and contains the finest row
of teeth in all this weary world. Her smile is emi-
nently intelligent. Her chin is full, and somewhat
heavy. All this is a tolerable catalogue, but no
picture. I have been tormenting my brain to discover whether it was her coloring or her form that
impressed me most. Fruitless speculation! Seriously, I think it was neither; it was her movement.
She walks a queen. It was the conscious poise of
her head, the unconscious "hang" of her arms, the
careless grace and dignity with which she lingered
along the garden-path, smelling a red red rose! She
has very little to say, apparently; but when she
speaks, it is to the point, and if the point suggests
it, with a very sweet smile. Indeed, if she is not
talkative, it is not from timidity. Is it from indifference? Time will elucidate this, as well as other
matters. I cling to the hypothesis that she is amiable. She is, moreover, intelligent; she is probably
quite reserved; and she is possibly very proud. She
is, in short, a woman of character. There you are,
Miss Blunt, at full length,—emphatically the portrait of a lady. After tea, she gave us some music
in the parlor. I confess that I was more taken with
the picture of the dusky little room, lighted by the
single candle on the piano, and by the *effect* of Miss
Blunt's performance, than with its meaning. She
appears to possess a very brilliant touch.

June 18th.—I have now been here almost a week. I occupy two very pleasant rooms. My painting-room is a vast and rather bare apartment, with a very good southern light. I have decked it out with a few old prints and sketches, and have already grown very fond of it. When I had disposed my artistic odds and ends in as picturesque a fashion as possible, I called in my hosts. The Captain looked about silently for some moments, and then inquired hopefully if I had ever tried my hand at a ship. On learning that I had not yet got to ships, he relapsed into a deferential silence. His daughter smiled and questioned very graciously, and called everything beautiful and delightful; which rather disappointed me, as I had taken her to be a woman of some originality. She is rather a puzzle;—or is she, indeed, a very commonplace person, and the fault in me, who am forever taking women to mean a great deal more than their Maker intended? Regarding Miss Blunt I have collected a few facts. She is not twenty-four, but twenty-seven years old. She has taught music ever since she was twenty, in a large boarding-school just out of the town, where she originally got her education. Her salary in this establishment, which is, I believe, a tolerably flourishing one, and the proceeds of a few additional lessons, constitute the chief revenues of the household. But Blunt fortunately owns his house, and his needs and habits are of the simplest kind. What does he or his daughter know of the great worldly theory of necessities, the great worldly scale of pleasures? Miss Blunt's only luxuries are a subscription to the circulating library, and an occasional walk on the beach, which, like one of Miss Brontë's heroines, she paces in company with an old Newfoundland dog. I am afraid she is sadly ignorant. She reads nothing but novels. I am bound to believe, however, that she has derived from the perusal of these works a certain practical science of her own. "I read all the novels I can get," she said yesterday; "but I only like the good ones. I do so like Zanoni, which I have just finished." I must set her to work at some of the masters. I should like some of those fretful New-York heiresses to see how this woman lives. I wish, too, that half a dozen of *ces messieurs* of the clubs might take a peep at the present way of life of their humble servant. We breakfast at eight o'clock. Immediately afterwards, Miss Blunt, in a shabby old bonnet and shawl, starts off to school. If the weather is fine, the Captain goes out a-fishing, and I am left to my own devices. Twice I have accompanied the old man. The second time I was lucky enough to catch a big bluefish, which we had for dinner. The Captain is an excellent specimen of the sturdy navigator, with his loose blue clothes, his ultra-divergent legs, his crisp white hair, and his jolly thick-skinned visage. He comes of a sea-faring English race. There is more or less of the ship's cabin in the general aspect of this antiquated house. I have heard the winds whistle about its walls, on two or three occasions, in true mid-ocean style. And then the illusion is heightened, somehow or other, by the extraordinary intensity of the light. My painting-room is a grand observatory of the clouds. I sit by the half-hour, watching them sail past my high, uncurtained windows. At the back part of the room, something tells you that they belong to an ocean sky; and there, in truth, as you draw nearer, you behold the vast, gray complement of sea. This quarter of the town is perfectly quiet. Human activity seems to have passed over it, never again to return, and to have left a kind of deposit of melancholy resignation. The streets are clean, bright, and airy; but this fact seems only to add to the intense sobriety. It implies that the unobstructed heavens are in the secret of their decline. There is something ghostly in the perpetual stillness. We frequently hear the rattling of the yards and the issuing of orders on the barks and schooners anchored out in the harbor.

June 28th.—My experiment works far better than I had hoped. I am thoroughly at my ease; my peace of mind quite passeth understanding. I work diligently; I have none but pleasant thoughts. The past has almost lost its terrors. For a week now I have been out sketching daily. The Captain carries me to a certain point on the shore of the harbor, I disembark and strike across the fields to a spot where I have established a kind of *rendezvous* with a particular effect of rock and shadow, which has been tolerably faithful to its appointment. Here I set up my easel, and paint till sunset. Then I retrace my steps and meet the boat. I am in every way much encouraged. The horizon of my work grows perceptibly wider. And then I am inexpressibly happy in the conviction that I am not wholly unfit for a life of (moderate) labor and (comparative) privation. I am quite in love with my poverty, if I may call it so. As why should I not? At this rate I don't spend eight hundred a year.

July 12th.—We have been having a week of bad weather: constant rain, night and day. This is certainly at once the brightest and the blackest spot in New England. The skies can smile, assuredly; but how they can frown! I have been painting rather languidly, and at a great disadvantage, at my window. . . . Through all this pouring and pattering, Miss Blunt sallies forth to her pupils. She envelops her beautiful head in a great woollen hood, her beautiful figure in a kind of feminine mackintosh; her feet she puts into heavy clogs, and over the whole she balances a cotton umbrella. When she comes home, with the rain-drops glistening on her red cheeks and her dark lashes, her cloak bespattered with mud, and her hands red with the cool damp, she is a profoundly wholesome spectacle. I never fail to make her a very low bow, for which she repays me with an extraordinary smile. This working-day side of her character is what especially pleases me in Miss Blunt. This holy working-dress of loveliness and dignity sits upon her with the simplicity of an antique drapery. Little use has she for whalebones and furbelows. What a poetry there is, after all, in red hands! I kiss yours, Mademoiselle. I do so because you are self-helpful; because you earn your living; because you are honest, simple, and ignorant (for a sensible woman, that is); because you speak and act to the point; because, in short, you are so unlike—certain of your sisters.

July 16th.—On Monday it cleared up generously. When I went to my window, on rising, I found sky and sea looking, for their brightness and freshness, like a clever English water-color. The ocean is of a deep purple blue; above it, the pure, bright sky looks pale, though it bends with an infinite depth over the inland horizon. Here and there on the

dark breezy water gleams the white cap of a wave,
or flaps the white cloak of a fishing-boat. I have
been sketching sedulously; I have discovered, within
a couple of miles' walk, a large, lonely pond, set in
quite a grand landscape of barren rocks and grassy
slopes. At one extremity is a broad outlook on the
open sea; at the other, deep buried in the foliage of
an apple-orchard, stands an old haunted-looking
farmhouse. To the west of the pond is a wide ex-
panse of rock and grass, of beach and marsh. The
sheep browse over it as upon a Highland moor.
Except a few stunted firs and cedars, there is not
a tree in sight. When I want shade, I seek it in the
shelter of one of the great mossy boulders which up-
heave their scintillating shoulders to the sun, or of
the long shallow dells where a tangle of blackberry-
bushes hedges about a sky-reflecting pool. I have
encamped over against a plain, brown hillside,
which, with laborious patience, I am transferring
to canvas; and as we have now had the same clear
sky for several days, I have almost finished quite
a satisfactory little study. I go forth immediately
after breakfast. Miss Blunt furnishes me with a
napkin full of bread and cold meat, which at the
noonday hour, in my sunny solitude, within sight
of the slumbering ocean, I voraciously convey to
my lips with my discolored fingers. At seven o'clock
I return to tea, at which repast we each tell the story

of our day's work. For poor Miss Blunt, it is day
after day the same story: a wearisome round of
visits to the school, and to the houses of the mayor,
the parson, the butcher, the baker, whose young ladies, of course, all receive instruction on the piano.
But she doesn't complain, nor, indeed, does she look
very weary. When she has put on a fresh calico
dress for tea, and arranged her hair anew, and with
these improvements flits about with that quiet
hither and thither of her gentle footsteps, preparing
our evening meal, peeping into the teapot, cutting
the solid loaf,—or when, sitting down on the low
door-step, she reads out select scraps from the evening paper,—or else, when, tea being over, she folds
her arms, (an attitude which becomes her mightily,)
and, still sitting on the door-step, gossips away the
evening in comfortable idleness, while her father
and I indulge in the fragrant pipe, and watch the
lights shining out, one by one, in different quarters
of the darkling bay: at these moments she is as
pretty, as cheerful, as careless as it becomes a sensible woman to be. What a pride the Captain takes
in his daughter! And she, in return, how perfect
is her devotion to the old man! He is proud of her
grace, of her tact, of her good sense, of her wit,
such as it is. He thinks her to be the most accomplished of women. He waits upon her as if, instead
of his old familiar Esther, she were a newly in-

ducted daughter-in-law. And indeed, if I were his
own son, he could not be kinder to me. They are
certainly—nay, why should I not say it?—*we* are
certainly a very happy little household. Will it last
forever? I say *we,* because both father and daughter have given me a hundred assurances—he direct,
and she, if I don't flatter myself, after the manner
of her sex, indirect—that I am already a valued
friend. It is natural enough that I should have
gained their good-will. They have received at my
hands inveterate courtesy. The way to the old
man's heart is through a studied consideration of
his daughter. He knows, I imagine, that I admire
Miss Blunt. But if I should at any time fall below
the mark of ceremony, I should have an account to
settle with him. All this is as it should be. When
people have to economize with the dollars and cents,
they have a right to be splendid in their feelings.
I have prided myself not a little on my good manners towards my hostess. That my bearing has been
without reproach is, however, a fact which I do not,
in any degree, set down here to my credit; for I
would defy the most impertinent of men (whoever
he is) to forget himself with this young lady, without leave unmistakably given. Those deep, dark
eyes have a strong prohibitory force. I record the
circumstance simply because in future years, when
my charming friend shall have become a distant

shadow, it will be pleasant, in turning over these pages, to find written testimony to a number of points which I shall be apt to charge solely upon my imagination. I wonder whether Miss Blunt, in days to come, referring to the tables of her memory for some trivial matter-of-fact, some prosaic date or half-buried landmark, will also encounter this little secret of ours, as I may call it,—will decipher an old faint note to this effect, overlaid with the memoranda of intervening years. Of course she will. Sentiment aside, she is a woman of an excellent memory. Whether she forgives or not I know not; but she certainly doesn't forget. Doubtless, virtue is its own reward; but there is a double satisfaction in being polite to a person on whom it *tells.* Another reason for my pleasant relations with the Captain is, that I afford him a chance to rub up his rusty old cosmopolitanism, and trot out his little scraps of old-fashioned reading, some of which are very curious. It is a great treat for him to spin his threadbare yarns over again to a sympathetic listener. These warm July evenings, in the sweet-smelling garden, are just the proper setting for his amiable garrulities. An odd enough relation subsists between us on this point. Like many gentlemen of his calling, the Captain is harassed by an irresistible desire to romance, even on the least promising themes; and it is vastly amusing to observe how he will auscultate, as it were, his auditor's inmost mood, to ascertain whether it is prepared for the absorption of his insidious fibs. Sometimes they perish utterly in the transition: they are very pretty, I conceive, in the deep and briny well of the Captain's fancy; but they won't bear being transplanted into the shallow inland lakes of my land-bred apprehension. At other times, the auditor being in a dreamy, sentimental, and altogether unprincipled mood, he will drink the old man's salt-water by the bucketful and feel none the worse for it. Which is the worse, wilfully to tell, or wilfully to believe, a pretty little falsehood which will not hurt any one? I suppose you can't believe wilfully; you only pretend to believe. My part of the game, therefore, is certainly as bad as the Captain's. Perhaps I take kindly to his beautiful perversions of fact, because I am myself engaged in one, because I am sailing under false colors of the deepest dye. I wonder whether my friends have any suspicion of the real state of the case. How should they? I fancy, that, on the whole, I play my part pretty well. I am delighted to find it come so easy. I do not mean that I experience little difficulty in foregoing my hundred petty elegancies and luxuries,—for to these, thank Heaven, I was not so indissolubly wedded that one wholesome shock could not loosen my bonds,—but that I manage more cleverly than I expected to stifle those innumerable tacit illusions which might serve effectually to belie my character.

Sunday, July 20th.—This has been a very pleasant day for me; although in it, of course, I have done no manner of work. I had this morning a delightful *tête-à-tête* with my hostess. She had sprained her ankle, coming downstairs; and so, instead of going forth to Sunday school and to meeting, she was obliged to remain at home on the sofa. The Captain, who is of a very punctilious piety, went off alone. When I came into the parlor, as the church-bells were ringing, Miss Blunt asked me if I never went to meeting. "Never when there is anything better to do at home," said I.

"What is better than going to church?" she asked, with charming simplicity.

She was reclining on the sofa, with her foot on a pillow, and her Bible in her lap. She looked by no means afflicted at having to be absent from divine service; and, instead of answering her question, I took the liberty of telling her so.

"I *am* sorry to be absent," said she. "You know it's my only festival in the week."

"So you look upon it as a festival," said I.

"Isn't it a pleasure to meet one's acquaintance? I confess I am never deeply interested in the ser-

mon, and I very much dislike teaching the children;
but I like wearing my best bonnet, and singing in
the choir, and walking part of the way home
with——"

"With whom?"

"With any one who offers to walk with me."

"With Mr. Johnson, for instance," said I.

Mr. Johnson is a young lawyer in the village,
who calls here once a week, and whose attentions to
Miss Blunt have been remarked.

"Yes," she answered, "Mr. Johnson will do as an
instance."

"How he will miss you!"

"I suppose he will. We sing off the same book.
What are you laughing at? He kindly permits me
to hold the book, while he stands with his hands in
his pockets. Last Sunday I quite lost patience.
'Mr. Johnson,' said I, 'do hold the book! Where
are your manners?' He burst out laughing in the
midst of the reading. He will certainly have to
hold the book to-day."

"What a 'masterful soul' he is! I suppose he will
call after meeting."

"Perhaps he will. I hope so."

"I hope he won't," said I, roundly. "I am going
to sit down here and talk to you, and I wish our
tête-à-tête not to be interrupted."

"Have you anything particular to say?"

"Nothing so particular as Mr. Johnson, perhaps."

Miss Blunt has a very pretty affectation of being more matter-of-fact than she really is.

"His rights, then," said she, "are paramount to yours."

"Ah, you admit that he has rights?"

"Not at all. I simply assert that you have none."

"I beg your pardon. I have claims which I mean to enforce. I have a claim upon your undivided attention, when I pay you a morning call."

"Your claim is certainly answered. Have I been uncivil, pray?"

"Not uncivil, perhaps, but inconsiderate. You have been sighing for the company of a third person, which you can't expect me to relish."

"Why not, pray? If I, a lady, can put up with Mr. Johnson's society, why shouldn't you, one of his own sex?"

"Because he is so outrageously conceited. You, as a lady, or at any rate as a woman, like conceited men."

"Ah, yes; I have no doubt that I, as a woman, have all kinds of improper tastes. That's an old story."

"Admit, at any rate, that our friend is conceited."

"Admit it? Why, I have said so a hundred times. I have told him so."

"Indeed! It has come to that, then?"

"To what, pray?"

"To that critical point in the friendship of a lady and gentleman, when they bring against each other all kinds of delightful charges of moral obliquity. Take care, Miss Blunt! A couple of intelligent New-Englanders, of opposite sex, young, unmarried, are pretty far gone, when they begin morally to reprobate each other. So you told Mr. Johnson that he is conceited? And I suppose you added, that he was also dreadfully satirical and skeptical? What was his rejoinder? Let me see. Did he ever tell you that you were a little bit affected?"

"No: he left that for you to say, in this very ingenious manner. Thank you, sir."

"He left it for me to deny, which is a great deal prettier. Do you think the manner ingenious?"

"I think the matter, considering the day and hour, very profane, Mr. Locksley. Suppose you go away and let me read my Bible."

"Meanwhile," I asked, "what shall I do?"

"Go and read yours, if you have one."

"I haven't."

I was, nevertheless, compelled to retire, with the promise of a second audience in half an hour. Poor Miss Blunt owes it to her conscience to read a certain number of chapters. What a pure and upright soul she is! And what an edifying spectacle is much of our feminine piety! Women find a place for everything in their commodious little minds, just as they do in their wonderfully subdivided trunks, when they go on a journey. I have no doubt that this young lady stows away her religion in a corner, just as she does her Sunday bonnet,—and, when the proper moment comes, draws it forth, and reflects while she assumes it before the glass, and blows away the strictly imaginary dust: for what worldly impurity can penetrate through half a dozen layers of cambric and tissue-paper? Dear me, what a comfort it is to have a nice, fresh, holiday faith!— When I returned to the parlor, Miss Blunt was still sitting with her Bible in her lap. Somehow or other, I no longer felt in the mood for jesting. So I asked her soberly what she had been reading. Soberly she answered me. She inquired how I had spent my half-hour.

"In thinking good Sabbath thoughts," I said. "I have been walking in the garden." And then I spoke my mind. "I have been thanking Heaven that it has led me, a poor, friendless wanderer, into so peaceful an anchorage."

"Are you, then, so poor and friendless?" asked Miss Blunt, quite abruptly.

"Did you ever hear of an art-student under thirty who wasn't poor?" I answered. "Upon my word, I have yet to sell my first picture. Then, as for being friendless, there are not five people in the world who really care for me."

"*Really* care? I am afraid you look too close. And then I think five good friends is a very large number. I think myself very well off with a couple. But if you are friendless, it's probably your own fault."

"Perhaps it is," said I, sitting down in the rocking-chair; "and yet, perhaps, it isn't. Have you found me so very repulsive? Haven't you, on the contrary, found me rather sociable?"

She folded her arms, and quietly looked at me for a moment, before answering. I shouldn't wonder if I blushed a little.

"You want a compliment, Mr. Locksley; that's the long and short of it. I have not paid you a compliment since you have been here. How you must have suffered! But it's a pity you couldn't have waited awhile longer, instead of beginning to angle with that very clumsy bait. For an artist, you are very inartistic. Men never know how to wait. 'Have I found you repulsive? haven't I found you sociable?' Perhaps, after all, considering what I have in my mind, it is as well that you asked for your compliment. I have found you charming. I say it freely; and yet I say, with equal sincerity, that I fancy very few others would find you so. I can say decidedly that you are not sociable. You are entirely too particular. You are considerate of me, because you know that I know that you are so. There's the rub, you see: I know that you know that I know it. Don't interrupt me; I am going to be eloquent. I want you to understand why I don't consider you sociable. You call Mr. Johnson conceited; but, really, I don't believe he's nearly as conceited as yourself. You are too conceited to be sociable; he is not. I am an obscure, weak-minded woman,—weak-minded, you know, compared with men. I can be patronized,—yes, that's the word. Would you be equally amiable with a person as strong, as clear-sighted as yourself, with a person equally averse with yourself to being under an obligation? I think not. Of course it's delightful to charm people. Who wouldn't? There is no harm in it, as long as the charmer does not set up for a public benefactor. If I were a man, a clever man like yourself, who had seen the world, who was not to be charmed and encouraged, but to be convinced and refuted, would you be equally amiable? It will perhaps seem absurd to you, and it will certainly seem egotistical, but I consider myself sociable, for all that I have only a couple of friends,—my father and the principal of the school. That is, I mingle with women without any second thought. Not that I wish you to do so: on the contrary, if the contrary is natural to you. But I don't believe you mingle in the same way with men. You may ask me what I know about it. Of course I know nothing: I simply guess. When I have done, indeed, I mean to beg your pardon for all I have said; but until then, give me a chance. You are incapable of listening deferentially to stupid, bigoted persons. I am not, I do it every day. Ah, you have no idea what nice manners I have in the exercise of my profession! Every day I have occasion to pocket my pride and to stifle my precious sense of the ridiculous,—of which, of course, you think I haven't a bit. It is, for instance, a constant vexation to me to be poor. It makes me frequently hate rich women; it makes me despise poor ones. I don't know whether you suffer acutely from the narrowness of your own means; but if you do, I dare say you shun rich men. I don't. I like to go into rich people's houses, and to be very polite to the ladies of the house, especially if they are very well-dressed and ignorant and vulgar. All women are like me in this respect; and all men more or less like you. That is, after all, the text of my sermon. Compared with us, it has always seemed to me that you are arrant cowards,—that we alone are brave. To be sociable, you must have a great deal of pluck. You are too fine a gentleman. Go and teach school, or open a corner grocery, or sit in a law-office all day, waiting for clients: *then* you will be sociable. As yet, you

are only agreeable. It *is* your own fault, if people
don't care for you. You don't care for them. That
you should be indifferent to their applause is all
very well; but you don't care for their indifference.
You are amiable, you are very kind, and you are
also very lazy. You consider that you are working now, don't you? Many persons would not call
it work."

It was now certainly my turn to fold my arms.

"And now," added my companion, as I did so,
"I beg your pardon."

"This was certainly worth waiting for," said I.
"I don't know what answer to make. My head
swims. I don't know whether you have been attack-
ing me or praising me. So you advise me to open
a corner grocery, do you?"

"I advise you to do something that will make you
a little less satirical. You had better marry, for
instance."

"*Je ne demande pas mieux.* Will you have me?
I can't afford it."

"Marry a rich woman."

I shook my head.

"Why not?" asked Miss Blunt. "Because people
would accuse you of being mercenary? What of
that? I mean to marry the first rich man who offers. Do you know that I am tired of living alone
in this weary old way, teaching little girls their

gamut, and turning and patching my dresses? I mean to marry the first man who offers."

"Even if he is poor?"

"Even if he is poor, ugly, and stupid."

"I am your man, then. Would you take me, if I were to offer?"

"Try and see."

"Must I get upon my knees?"

"No, you need not even do that. Am I not on mine? It would be too fine an irony. Remain as you are, lounging back in your chair, with your thumbs in your waistcoat."

If I were writing a romance now, instead of transcribing facts, I would say that I knew not what might have happened at this juncture, had not the door opened and admitted the Captain and Mr. Johnson. The latter was in the highest spirits.

"How are you, Miss Esther? So you have been breaking your leg, eh? How are you, Mr. Locksley? I wish I were a doctor now. Which is it, right or left?"

In this simple fashion he made himself agreeable to Miss Blunt. He stopped to dinner and talked without ceasing. Whether our hostess had talked herself out in her very animated address to myself an hour before, or whether she preferred to oppose no obstacle to Mr. Johnson's fluency, or whether she was indifferent to him, I know not; but she held her tongue with that easy grace, that charming tacit intimation of "We could, and we would," of which she is so perfect a mistress. This very interesting woman has a number of pretty traits in common with her town-bred sisters; only, whereas in these they are laboriously acquired, in her they are severely natural. I am sure, that, if I were to plant her in Madison Square to-morrow, she would, after one quick, all-compassing glance, assume the *nil admirari* in a manner to drive the greatest lady of them all to despair. Johnson is a man of excellent intentions, but no taste. Two or three times I looked at Miss Blunt to see what impression his sallies were making upon her. They seemed to produce none whatever. But I know better, *moi*. Not one of them escaped her. But I suppose she said to herself that her impressions on this point were no business of mine. Perhaps she was right. It is a disagreeable word to use of a woman you admire; but I can't help fancying that she has been a little *soured*. By what? Who shall say? By some old love affair, perhaps.

July 24th.—This evening the Captain and I took a half-hour's turn about the harbor. I asked him frankly, as a friend, whether Johnson wants to marry his daughter.

"I guess he does," said the old man; "and yet I

hope he don't. You know what he is: he's smart, promising, and already sufficiently well off. But somehow he isn't for a man what my Esther is for a woman."

"That he isn't!" said I; "and honestly, Captain Blunt, I don't know who is——"

"Unless it's yourself," said the Captain.

"Thank you. I know a great many ways in which Mr. Johnson is more worthy of her than I."

"And I know one in which you are more worthy of her than he,—that is, in being what we used to call a gentleman."

"Miss Esther made him sufficiently welcome in her quiet way, on Sunday," I rejoined.

"Oh, she respects him," said Blunt. "As she's situated, she might marry him on that. You see, she's weary of hearing little girls drum on the piano. With her ear for music," added the Captain, "I wonder she has borne it so long."

"She is certainly meant for better things," said I.

"Well," answered the Captain, who has an honest habit of deprecating your agreement, when it occurs to him that he has obtained it for sentiments which fall somewhat short of the stoical,—"well," said he, with a very dry expression of mouth, "she's born to do her duty. We are all of us born for that."

"Sometimes our duty is rather dreary," said I.

"So it be; but what's the help for it? I don't want to die without seeing my daughter provided for. What she makes by teaching is a pretty slim subsistence. There was a time when I thought she was going to be fixed for life, but it all blew over. There was a young fellow here from down Boston way, who came about as near to it as you can come, when you actually don't. He and Esther were excellent friends. One day Esther came up to me, and looked me in the face, and told me she was engaged.

" 'Who to?' says I, though, of course, I knew, and Esther told me as much. 'When do you expect to marry?' I asked.

" 'When John grows rich enough,' says she.

" 'When will that be?'

" 'It may not be for years,' said poor Esther.

"A whole year passed, and, as far as I could see, the young man came no nearer to his fortune. He was forever running to and fro between this place and Boston. I asked no questions, because I knew that my poor girl wished it so. But at last, one day, I began to think it was time to take an observation, and see whereabouts we stood.

" 'Has John made his fortune yet?' I asked.

" 'I don't know, father,' said Esther.

" 'When are you to be married?'

" 'Never!' said my poor little girl, and burst into

tears. 'Please ask me no questions,' said she. 'Our engagement is over. Ask me no questions.'

" 'Tell me one thing,' said I: 'where is that d—d scoundrel who has broken my daughter's heart?'

"You should have seen the look she gave me.

" 'Broken my heart, sir? You are very much mistaken. I don't know who you mean.'

" 'I mean John Banister,' said I. That was his name.

" 'I believe Mr. Banister is in China,' says Esther, as grand as the Queen of Sheba. And there was an end of it. I never learnt the ins and outs of it. I have been told that Banister is accumulating money very fast in the China trade."

August 7th.—I have made no entry for more than a fortnight. They tell me I have been very ill; and I find no difficulty in believing them. I suppose I took cold, sitting out so late, sketching. At all events, I have had a mild intermittent fever. I have slept so much, however, that the time has seemed rather short. I have been tenderly nursed by this kind old gentleman, his daughter, and his maid-servant. God bless them, one and all! I say his daughter, because old Dorothy informs me that for half an hour one morning, at dawn, after a night during which I had been very feeble, Miss Blunt relieved guard at my bedside, while I lay

wrapt in brutal slumber. It is very jolly to see sky
and ocean once again. I have got myself into my
easy-chair by the open window, with my shutters
closed and the lattice open; and here I sit with my
book on my knee, scratching away feebly enough.
Now and then I peep from my cool, dark sick-cham-
ber out into the world of light. High noon at mid-
summer! What a spectacle! There are no clouds
in the sky, no waves on the ocean. The sun has it
all to himself. To look long at the garden makes
the eyes water. And we—"Hobbs, Nobbs, Stokes,
and Nokes"—propose to paint that kingdom of light.
Allons, donc!

The loveliest of women has just tapped, and
come in with a plate of early peaches. The peaches
are of a gorgeous color and plumpness; but Miss
Blunt looks pale and thin. The hot weather doesn't
agree with her. She is overworked. Confound it!
Of course I thanked her warmly for her attentions
during my illness. She disclaims all gratitude, and
refers me to her father and Mrs. Dorothy.

"I allude more especially," said I, "to that little
hour at the end of a weary night, when you stole in
like a kind of moral Aurora, and drove away the
shadows from my brain. That morning, you know,
I began to get better."

"It was, indeed, a very little hour," said Miss
Blunt. "It was about ten minutes." And then she

began to scold me for presuming to touch a pen during my convalescence. She laughs at me, indeed, for keeping a diary at all. "Of all things," cried she, "a sentimental man is the most despicable."

I confess I was somewhat nettled. The thrust seemed gratuitous.

"Of all things," I answered, "a woman without sentiment is the most unlovely."

"Sentiment and loveliness are all very well, when you have time for them," said Miss Blunt. "I haven't. I'm not rich enough. Good morning."

Speaking of another woman, I would say that she flounced out of the room. But such was the gait of Juno, when she moved stiffly over the grass from where Paris stood with Venus holding the apple, gathering up her divine vestment, and leaving the others to guess at her face——

Juno has just come back to say that she forgot what she came for half an hour ago. What will I be pleased to like for dinner?

"I have just been writing in my diary that you flounced out of the room," said I.

"Have you, indeed? Now you can write that I have bounced in. There's a nice cold chicken downstairs," etc., etc.

August 14th.—This afternoon I sent for a light

wagon, and treated Miss Blunt to a drive. We went successively over the three beaches. What a time we had, coming home! I shall never forget that hard trot over Weston's Beach. The tide was very low; and we had the whole glittering, weltering strand to ourselves. There was a heavy blow yesterday, which had not yet subsided; and the waves had been lashed into a magnificent fury. Trot, trot, trot, trot, we trundled over the hard sand. The sound of the horse's hoofs rang out sharp against the monotone of the thunderous surf, as we drew nearer and nearer to the long line of the cliffs. At our left, almost from the lofty zenith of the pale evening sky to the high western horizon of the tumultuous dark-green sea, was suspended, so to speak, one of those gorgeous vertical sunsets that Turner loved so well. It was a splendid confusion of purple and green and gold,—the clouds flying and flowing in the wind like the folds of a mighty banner borne by some triumphal fleet whose prows were not visible above the long chain of mountainous waves. As we reached the point where the cliffs plunge down upon the beach, I pulled up, and we remained for some moments looking out along the low, brown, obstinate barrier at whose feet the impetuous waters were rolling themselves into powder.

August 17th.—This evening, as I lighted my bedroom candle, I saw that the Captain had something to say to me. So I waited below until the old man and his daughter had performed their usual picturesque embrace, and the latter had given me that hand-shake and that smile which I never failed to exact.

"Johnson has got his discharge," said the old man, when he had heard his daughter's door close upstairs.

"What do you mean?"

He pointed with his thumb to the room above, where we heard, through the thin partition, the movement of Miss Blunt's light step.

"You mean that he has proposed to Miss Esther?"

The Captain nodded.

"And has been refused?"

"Flat."

"Poor fellow!" said I, very honestly. "Did he tell you himself?"

"Yes, with tears in his eyes. He wanted me to speak for him. I told him it was no use. Then he began to say hard things of my poor girl."

"What kind of things?"

"A pack of falsehoods. He says she has no heart. She has promised always to regard him as a friend: it's more than I will, hang him!"

"Poor fellow!" said I; and now, as I write, I

can only repeat, considering what a hope was here broken, Poor fellow!

August 23d.—I have been lounging about all day, thinking of it, dreaming of it, spooning over it, as they say. This is a decided waste of time. I think, accordingly, the best thing for me to do is, to sit down and lay the ghost by writing out my story.

On Thursday evening Miss Blunt happened to intimate that she had a holiday on the morrow, it being the birthday of the lady in whose establishment she teaches.

"There is to be a tea-party at four o'clock in the afternoon for the resident pupils and teachers," said Miss Esther. "Tea at four! what do you think of that? And then there is to be a speech-making by the smartest young lady. As my services are not required, I propose to be absent. Suppose, father, you take us out in your boat. Will you come, Mr. Locksley? We shall have a nice little picnic. Let us go over to old Fort Pudding, across the bay. We will take our dinner with us, and send Dorothy to spend the day with her sister, and put the house-key in our pocket, and not come home till we please."

I warmly espoused the project, and it was accordingly carried into execution the next morning, when, at about ten o'clock, we pushed off from our little wharf at the garden-foot. It was a perfect summer's day: I can say no more for it. We made a quiet run over to the point of our destination. I shall never forget the wondrous stillness which brooded over earth and water, as we weighed anchor in the lee of my old friend,—or old enemy,— the ruined fort. The deep, translucent water reposed at the base of the warm sunlit cliff like a great basin of glass, which I half expected to hear shiver and crack as our keel ploughed through it. And how color and sound stood out in the transparent air! How audibly the little ripples on the beach whispered to the open sky! How our irreverent voices seemed to jar upon the privacy of the little cove! The mossy rocks doubled themselves without a flaw in the clear, dark water. The gleaming white beach lay fringed with its deep deposits of odorous sea-weed, gleaming black. The steep, straggling sides of the cliffs raised aloft their rugged angles against the burning blue of the sky. I remember, when Miss Blunt stepped ashore and stood upon the beach, relieved against the heavy shadow of a recess in the cliff, while her father and I busied ourselves with gathering up our baskets and fastening the anchor—I remember, I say, what a figure she made. There is a certain purity in this Cragthorpe air which I have never seen approached, —a lightness, a brilliancy, a *crudity,* which allows perfect liberty of self-assertion to each individual object in the landscape. The prospect is ever more or less like a picture which lacks its final process, its reduction to unity. Miss Blunt's figure, as she stood there on the beach, was almost *criarde;* but how lovely it was! Her light muslin dress, gathered up over her short white skirt, her little black mantilla, the blue veil which she had knotted about her neck, the crimson shawl which she had thrown over her arm, the little silken dome which she poised over her head in one gloved hand, while the other retained her crisp draperies, and which cast down upon her face a sharp circle of shade, out of which her cheerful eyes shone darkly and her happy mouth smiled whitely,—these are some of the hastily noted points of the picture.

"Young woman," I cried out, over the water, "I do wish you might know how pretty you look!"

"How do you know I don't?" she answered. "I should think I might. You don't look so badly, yourself. But it's not I; it's the accessories."

"Hang it! I am going to become profane," I called out again.

"Swear ahead," said the Captain.

"I am going to say you are devilish pretty."

"Dear me! is that all?" cried Miss Blunt, with a little light laugh, which must have made the tutelar sirens of the cove ready to die with jealousy down in their submarine bowers.

By the time the Captain and I had landed our effects, our companion had tripped lightly up the forehead of the cliff—in one place it is very retreating—and disappeared over its crown. She soon reappeared with an intensely white handkerchief added to her other provocations, which she waved to us, as we trudged upward, carrying our baskets. When we stopped to take breath on the summit, and wipe our foreheads, we, of course, rebuked her who was roaming about idly with her parasol and gloves.

"Do you think I am going to take any trouble or do any work?" cried Miss Esther, in the greatest good-humor. "Is not this my holiday? I am not going to raise a finger, nor soil these beautiful gloves, for which I paid a dollar at Mr. Dawson's in Cragthorpe. After you have found a shady place for your provisions, I would like you to look for a spring. I am very thirsty."

"Find the spring yourself, Miss," said her father. "Mr. Locksley and I have a spring in this basket. Take a pull, sir."

And the Captain drew forth a stout black bottle.

"Give me a cup, and I will look for some water," said Miss Blunt. "Only I'm so afraid of the snakes! If you hear a scream, you may know it's a snake."

"Screaming snakes!" said I; "that's a new species."

What nonsense it all sounds like now! As we

looked about us, shade seemed scarce, as it generally is, in this region. But Miss Blunt, like the very adroit and practical young person she is, for all that she would have me believe the contrary, soon discovered a capital cool spring in the shelter of a pleasant little dell, beneath a clump of firs. Hither, as one of the young gentlemen who imitate Tennyson would say, we brought our basket, Blunt and I; while Esther dipped the cup, and held it dripping to our thirsty lips, and laid the cloth, and on the grass disposed the platters round. I should have to be a poet, indeed, to describe half the happiness and the silly poetry and purity and beauty of this bright long summer's day. We ate, drank, and talked; we ate occasionally with our fingers, we drank out of the necks of our bottles, and we talked with our mouths full, as befits (and excuses) those who talk wild nonsense. We told stories without the least point. Blunt and I made atrocious puns. I believe, indeed, that Miss Blunt herself made one little punkin, as I called it. If there had been any superfluous representative of humanity present, to register the fact, I should say that we made fools of ourselves. But as there was no fool on hand, I need say nothing about it. I am conscious myself of having said several witty things, which Miss Blunt understood: *in vino veritas*. The dear old Captain twanged the long bow indefatigably. The bright high sun lingered above us the livelong day, and drowned the prospect with light and warmth. One of these days I mean to paint a picture which in future ages, when my dear native land shall boast a national school of art, will hang in the *Salon Carré* of the great central museum, (located, let us say, in Chicago,) and remind folks—or rather make them forget—Giorgione, Bordone, and Veronese: A Rural Festival; three persons feasting under some trees; scene, nowhere in particular; time and hour, problematical. Female figure, a big *brune;* young man reclining on his elbow; old man drinking. An empty sky, with no end of expression. The whole stupendous in color, drawing, feeling. Artist uncertain; supposed to be Robinson, 1900. That's about the programme.

After dinner the Captain began to look out across the bay, and, noticing the uprising of a little breeze, expressed a wish to cruise about for an hour or two. He proposed to us to walk along the shore to a point a couple of miles northward, and there meet the boat. His daughter having agreed to this proposition, he set off with the lightened pannier, and in less than half an hour we saw him standing out from shore. Miss Blunt and I did not begin our walk for a long, long time. We sat and talked beneath the trees. At our feet, a wide cleft in the hills—almost a glen—stretched down to the silent beach. Beyond lay the familiar ocean-line. But, as many philosophers have observed, there is an end to all things. At last we got up. Miss Blunt said, that, as the air was freshening, she believed she would put on her shawl. I helped her to fold it into the proper shape, and then I placed it on her shoulders, her crimson shawl over her black silk sack. And then she tied her veil once more about her neck, and gave me her hat to hold, while she effected a partial redistribution of her hair-pins. By way of being humorous, I placed her hat on my own head; at which she was kind enough to smile, as with downcast face and uplifted elbows she fumbled among her braids. And then she shook out the creases of her dress, and drew on her gloves; and finally she said, "Well!"—that inevitable tribute to time and morality which follows upon even the mildest form of dissipation. Very slowly it was that we wandered down the little glen. Slowly, too, we followed the course of the narrow and sinuous beach, as it keeps to the foot of the low cliffs. We encountered no sign of human interest. Our conversation I need hardly repeat. I think I may trust it to the keeping of my memory; I think I shall be likely to remember it. It was all very sober and sensible,—such talk as it is both easy and pleasant to remember; it was even prosaic,—or, at least, if there was a vein of poetry in it, I should have defied

a listener to put his finger on it. There was no ex-
altation of feeling or utterance on either side; on
one side, indeed, there was very little utterance. Am
I wrong in conjecturing, however, that there was
considerable feeling of a certain quiet kind? Miss
Blunt maintained a rich, golden silence. I, on the
other hand, was very voluble. What a sweet, womanly listener she is!

September 1st.—I have been working steadily for
a week. This is the first day of autumn. Read
aloud to Miss Blunt a little Wordsworth.

September 10th. Midnight.—Worked without
interruption,—until yesterday, inclusive, that is.
But with the day now closing—or opening—begins
a new era. My poor vapid old diary, at last you
shall hold a *fact.*

For three days past we have been having damp,
chilly weather. Dusk has fallen early. This evening, after tea, the Captain went into town,—on business, as he said: I believe, to attend some Poor-
house or Hospital Board. Esther and I went into
the parlor. The room seemed cold. She brought
in the lamp from the dining-room, and proposed we
should have a little fire. I went into the kitchen,
procured an armful of wood, and while she drew
the curtains and wheeled up the table, I kindled a

lively, crackling blaze. A fortnight ago she would not have allowed me to do this without a protest. She would not have offered to do it herself,—not she!—but she would have said that I was not here to serve, but to be served, and would have pretended to call Dorothy. Of course I should have had my own way. But we have changed all that. Esther went to her piano, and I sat down to a book. I read not a word. I sat looking at my mistress, and thinking with a very uneasy heart. For the first time in our friendship, she had put on a dark, warm dress: I think it was of the material called alpaca. The first time I saw her she wore a white dress with a purple neck-ribbon; now she wore a black dress with the same ribbon. That is, I remember wondering, as I sat there eyeing her, whether it *was* the same ribbon, or merely another like it. My heart was in my throat; and yet I thought of a number of trivialities of the same kind. At last I spoke.

"Miss Blunt," I said, "do you remember the first evening I passed beneath your roof, last June?"

"Perfectly," she replied, without stopping.

"You played this same piece."

"Yes; I played it very badly, too. I only half knew it. But it is a showy piece, and I wished to produce an effect. I didn't know then how indifferent you are to music."

"I paid no particular attention to the piece. I was intent upon the performer."

"So the performer supposed."

"What reason had you to suppose so?"

"I'm sure I don't know. Did you ever know a woman to be able to give a reason, when she has guessed aright?"

"I think they generally contrive to make up a reason, afterwards. Come, what was yours?"

"Well, you *stared* so hard."

"Fie! I don't believe it. That's unkind."

"You said you wished me to invent a reason. If I really had one, I don't remember it."

"You told me you remembered the occasion in question perfectly."

"I meant the circumstances. I remember what we had for tea; I remember what dress I wore. But I don't remember my feelings. They were naturally not very memorable."

"What did you say, when your father proposed my coming?"

"I asked how much you would be willing to pay."

"And then?"

"And then, if you looked 'respectable'."

"And then?"

"That was all. I told father that he could do as he pleased."

She continued to play. Leaning back in my chair,

I continued to look at her. There was a considerable pause.

"Miss Esther," said I, at last.

"Yes."

"Excuse me for interrupting you so often. But," —and I got up and went to the piano,—"but I thank Heaven that it has brought you and me together."

She looked up at me and bowed her head with a little smile, as her hands still wandered over the keys.

"Heaven has certainly been very good to us," said she.

"How much longer are you going to play?" I asked.

"I'm sure I don't know. As long as you like."

"If you want to do as I like, you will stop immediately."

She let her hands rest on the keys a moment, and gave me a rapid, questioning look. Whether she found a sufficient answer in my face I know not; but she slowly rose, and, with a very pretty affectation of obedience, began to close the instrument. I helped her to do so.

"Perhaps you would like to be quite alone," she said. "I suppose your own room is too cold."

"Yes," I answered, "you've hit it exactly. I wish to be alone. I wish to monopolize this cheerful blaze. Hadn't you better go into the kitchen and sit with the cook? It takes you women to make such cruel speeches."

"When we women are cruel, Mr. Locksley, it is without knowing it. We are not wilfully so. When we learn that we have been unkind, we very humbly ask pardon, without even knowing what our crime has been." And she made me a very low curtsy.

"I will tell you what your crime has been," said I. "Come and sit by the fire. It's rather a long story."

"A long story? Then let me get my work."

"Confound your work! Excuse me, but I mean it. I want you to listen to me. Believe me, you will need all your thoughts."

She looked at me steadily a moment, and I returned her glance. During that moment I was reflecting whether I might silently emphasize my request by laying a lover's hand upon her shoulder. I decided that I might not. She walked over and quietly seated herself in a low chair by the fire. Here she patiently folded her arms. I sat down before her.

"With you, Miss Blunt," said I, "one must be very explicit. You are not in the habit of taking things for granted. You have a great deal of imagination, but you rarely exercise it on the behalf of other people." I stopped a moment.

"Is that my crime?" asked my companion.

"It's not so much a crime as a vice," said I; "and perhaps not so much a vice as a virtue. Your crime is, that you are so stone-cold to a poor devil who loves you."

She burst into a rather shrill laugh. I wonder whether she thought I meant Johnson.

"Who are you speaking for, Mr. Locksley?" she asked.

"Are there so many? For myself."

"Honestly?"

"Honestly doesn't begin to express it."

"What is that French phrase that you are forever using? I think I may say, *'Allons, donc!'* "

"Let us speak plain English, Miss Blunt."

" 'Stone-cold' is certainly very plain English. I don't see the relative importance of the two branches of your proposition. Which is the principal, and which the subordinate clause,—that I am stone-cold, as you call it, or that you love me, as you call it?"

"As I call it? What would you have me call it? For God's sake, Miss Blunt, be serious, or I shall call it something else. Yes, I love you. Don't you believe it?"

"I am open to conviction."

"Thank God!" said I.

And I attempted to take her hand.

"No, no, Mr. Locksley," said she,—"not just yet; if you please."

"Action speaks louder than words," said I.

"There is no need of speaking loud. I hear you perfectly."

"I certainly sha'n't whisper," said I; "although it is the custom, I believe, for lovers to do so. Will you be my wife?"

"I sha'n't whisper, either, Mr. Locksley. Yes, I will."

And now she put out her hand.—That's my fact.

September 12th.—We are to be married within three weeks.

September 19th.—I have been in New York a week, transacting business. I got back yesterday. I find every one here talking about our engagement. Esther tells me that it was talked about a month ago, and that there is a very general feeling of disappointment that I am not rich.

"Really, if you don't mind it," said I, "I don't see why others should."

"I don't know whether you are rich or not," says Esther; "but I know that I am."

"Indeed! I was not aware that you had a private fortune," etc., etc.

This little farce is repeated in some shape every day. I am very idle. I smoke a great deal, and lounge about all day, with my hands in my pockets. I am free from that ineffable weariness of ceaseless *giving* which I experienced six months ago. I was shorn of my hereditary trinkets at that period; and I have resolved that *this* engagement, at all events, shall have no connection with the shops. I was balked of my poetry once; I sha'n't be a second time. I don't think there is much danger of this. Esther deals it out with full hands. She takes a very pretty interest in her simple outfit,—showing me triumphantly certain of her purchases, and making a great mystery about others, which she is pleased to denominate table-cloths and napkins. Last evening I found her sewing buttons on a table-cloth. I had heard a great deal of a certain gray silk dress; and this morning, accordingly, she marched up to me, arrayed in this garment. It is trimmed with velvet, and hath flounces, a train, and all the modern improvements generally.

"There is only one objection to it," said Esther, parading before the glass in my painting-room: "I am afraid it is above our station."

"By Jove! I'll paint your portrait in it," said I, "and make our fortune. All the other men who have handsome wives will bring them to be painted."

"You mean all the women who have handsome dresses," said Esther, with great humility.

Our wedding is fixed for next Thursday. I tell Esther that it will be as little of a wedding, and as much of a marriage, as possible. Her father and her good friend the schoolmistress alone are to be present.—My secret oppresses me considerably; but I have resolved to keep it for the honeymoon, when it may take care of itself. I am harassed with a dismal apprehension, that, if Esther were to discover it now, the whole thing would be *à refaire*. I have taken rooms at a romantic little watering-place called Clifton, ten miles off. The hotel is already quite free of city-people, and we shall be almost alone.

September 28th.—We have been here two days. The little transaction in the church went off smoothly. I am truly sorry for the Captain. We drove directly over here, and reached the place at dusk. It was a raw, black day. We have a couple of good rooms, close to the savage sea. I am nevertheless afraid I have made a mistake. It would perhaps have been wiser to go inland. These things are not immaterial: we make our own heaven, but we scarcely make our own earth. I am writing at a little table by the window, looking out on the rocks, the gathering dusk, and the rising fog. My wife has wandered down to the rocky platform in front of the house. I can see her from here, bareheaded, in that old crimson shawl, talking to one of the landlord's little boys. She has just given the little fellow a kiss, bless her heart! I remember her telling me once that she was very fond of little boys; and, indeed, I have noticed that they are seldom too dirty for her to take on her knee. I have been reading over these pages for the first time in—I don't know when. They are filled with *her,*—even more in thought than in word. I believe I will show them to her, when she comes in. I will give her the book to read, and sit by her, watching her face,—watching the great secret dawn upon her.

Later.—Somehow or other, I can write this quietly enough; but I hardly think I shall ever write any more. When Esther came in, I handed her this book.

"I want you to read it," said I.

She turned very pale, and laid it on the table, shaking her head.

"I know it," she said.

"What do you know?"

"That you have a hundred thousand a year. But, believe me, Mr. Locksley, I am none the worse for the knowledge. You intimated in one place in your book that I am born for wealth and splendor. I believe I am. You pretend to hate your money; but you would not have had me without it. If you really love me,—and I think you do,—you will not let this make any difference. I am not such a fool as to attempt to talk here about my sensations. But I remember what I said."

"What do you expect me to do?" I asked. "Shall I call you some horrible name and cast you off?"

"I expect you to show the same courage that I am showing. I never said I loved you. I never deceived you in that. I said I would be your wife. So I will, faithfully. I haven't so much heart as you think; and yet, too, I have a great deal more. I am incapable of more than one deception.— Mercy! didn't you see it? didn't you know it? see that I saw it? know that I knew it? It was diamond cut diamond. You deceived me; I deceived you. Now that your deception ceases, mine ceases. *Now* we are free, with our hundred thousand a year! Excuse me, but it sometimes comes across me! *Now* we can be good and honest and true. It was all a make-believe virtue before."

"So you read that thing?" I asked: actually— strange as it may seem—for something to say.

"Yes, while you were ill. It was lying with your pen in it, on the table. I read it because I suspected. Otherwise I shouldn't have done so."

"It was the act of a false woman," said I.

"A false woman? No,—simply of a woman. I am a woman, sir." And she began to smile. "Come, *you* be a man!"

II

POOR RICHARD

A Story in Three Parts

PART I

Miss Whittaker's garden covered a couple of acres, behind and beside her house, and at its farther extremity was bounded by a narrow meadow, which in turn was bordered by the old, disused towing-path beside the river, at this point a slow and shallow stream. Its low, flat banks were unadorned with rocks or trees, and a towing-path is not in itself a romantic promenade. Nevertheless, here sauntered bareheaded, on a certain spring evening, the mistress of the acres just mentioned and many more beside, in sentimental converse with an impassioned and beautiful youth.

She herself had been positively plain, but for the frequent recurrence of a magnificent broad smile,— which imparted loveliness to her somewhat plebeian features,—and (in another degree) for the elegance of her dress, which expressed one of the later stages of mourning, and was of that voluminous abundance proper to women who are massive in person, and rich besides. Her companion's good looks, for very good they were, in spite of several defects, were set off by a shabby suit, as carelessly worn as it was inartistically cut. His manner, as he walked and talked, was that of a nervous, passionate man, wrought almost to desperation; while her own was that of a person self-composed to generous attention. A brief silence, however, had at last fallen upon them. Miss Whittaker strolled along quietly, looking at the slow-mounting moon, and the young man gazed on the ground, swinging his stick. Finally, with a heavy blow, he brought it to earth.

"O Gertrude!" he cried, "I despise myself."

"That's very foolish," said Gertrude.

"And, Gertrude, I adore you."

"That's more foolish still," said Gertrude, with her eyes still on the moon. And then, suddenly and somewhat impatiently transferring them to her companion's face, "Richard," she asked, "what do you mean when you say you adore me?"

"Mean? I mean that I love you."

"Then, why don't you say what you mean?"

The young man looked at her a moment. "Will you give me leave," he asked, "to say *all* that I mean?"

"Of course." Then, as he remained silent, "I listen," added Gertrude.

Yet he still said nothing, but went striking ve-
hemently at the weeds by the water's edge, like one
who may easily burst into tears of rage.

"Gertrude!" he suddenly exclaimed, "what more
do you want than the assurance that I love you?"

"I want nothing more. That assurance is by itself delightful enough. You yourself seemed to
wish to add something more."

"Either you won't understand me," cried Richard, "or"—flagrantly vicious for twenty seconds—
"you can't!"

Miss Whittaker stopped and looked thoughtfully
into his face. "In our position," she said, "if it
becomes you to sacrifice reflection to feeling, it becomes me to do the reverse. Listen to me, Richard.
I *do* understand you, and better, I fancy, than you
understand yourself."

"O, of course!"

But she continued, heedless of his interruption.
"I thought that, by leaving you to yourself awhile,
your feelings might become clearer to you. But
they seem to be growing only more confused. I
have been so fortunate, or so unfortunate, I hardly
know which,"—and she smiled faintly,—"as to
please you. That's all very well, but you must not
make too much of it. Nothing can make me happier than to please you, or to please any one. But
here it must stop with you, as it stops with others."

"It does not stop here with others."

"I beg your pardon. You have no right to say that. It is partly out of justice to others that I speak to you as I am doing. I shall always be one of your best friends, but I shall never be more. It is best I should tell you this at once. I might trifle with you awhile and make you happy (since upon such a thing you are tempted to set your happiness) by allowing you to suppose that I had given you my heart; but the end would soon come, and then where should we be? You may in your disappointment call me heartless now,—I freely give you leave to call me anything that may ease your mind,—but what would you call me then? Friendship, Richard, is a heavenly cure for love. Here is mine," and she held out her hand.

"No, I thank you," said Richard, gloomily folding his arms. "I know my own feelings," and he raised his voice. "Haven't I lived with them night and day for weeks and weeks? Great Heaven, Gertrude, this is no fancy. I'm not of that sort. My whole life has gone into my love. God has let me idle it away hitherto, only that I might begin it with you. Dear Gertrude, hear me. I have the heart of a man. I know I'm not respectable, but I devoutly believe I'm lovable. It's true that I've neither worked, nor thought, nor studied, nor turned a penny. But, on the other hand, I've never cared for a woman before. I've waited for you. And now—now, after all, I'm to sit down and be *pleased!* The Devil! Please other men, madam! Me·you delight, you intoxicate."

An honest flush rose to Gertrude's cheek. "So much the worse for you!" she cried with a bitter laugh. "So much the worse for both of us! But what is your point? Do you wish to marry me?"

Richard flinched a moment under this tacit proposition suddenly grown vocal; but not from want of heart. "Of course I do," he said.

"Well, then, I only pity you the more for your consistency. I can only entreat you again to rest contented with my friendship. It's not such a bad substitute, Richard, as I understand it. What my love might be I don't know,—I couldn't answer for that; but of my friendship I'm sure. We both have our duties in this matter, and I have resolved to take a liberal view of mine. I might lose patience with you, you know, and dismiss you,—leave you alone with your dreams, and let you break your heart. But it's rather by seeing more of me than by seeing less, that your feelings will change."

"Indeed! And yours?"

"I have no doubt they will change, too; not in kind, but in degree. The better I know you, I am sure, the better I shall like you. The better, too, you will like me. Don't turn your back upon me.

I speak the truth. You will get to entertain a serious opinion of me,—which I'm sure you haven't now, or you wouldn't talk of my intoxicating you. But you must be patient. It's a singular fact that it takes longer to like a woman than to love her. A sense of intoxication is a very poor feeling to marry upon. You wish, of course, to break with your idleness, and your bad habits,—you see I am so thoroughly your friend that I'm not afraid of touching upon disagreeable facts, as I should be if I were your mistress. But you are so indolent, so irresolute, so undisciplined, so uneducated,"—Gertrude spoke deliberately, and watched the effect of her words,— "that you find a change of life very difficult. I propose, with your consent, to appoint myself your counsellor. Henceforth my house will be open to you as to my dearest friend. Come as often and stay as long as you please. Not in a few weeks, perhaps, nor even in a few months, but in God's good time, you will be a noble young man in working order,—which I don't consider you now, and which I know you don't consider yourself. But I have a great opinion of your talents," (this was very shrewd of Gertrude,) "and of your heart. If I turn out to have done you a service, you'll not want to marry me then."

Richard had silently listened, with a deepening frown. "That's all very pretty," he said; "but"—

and the reader will see that, in his earnestness, he
was inclined to dispense with courtesy—"it's rotten,
—rotten from beginning to end. What's the meaning of all that rigmarole about the inconsistency of
friendship and love? Such talk is enough to drive
one mad. Refuse me outright, and send me to the
Devil if you must; but don't bemuddle your own
brains at the same time. But one little word knocks
it all to pieces: I want you for my wife. You make
an awful mistake in treating me as a boy,—an awful
mistake. I *am* in working order. I have begun life
in loving you. I have broken with drinking as effectually as if I hadn't touched a drop of liquor for
twenty years. I hate it, I loathe it. I've drunk
my last. No, Gertrude, I'm no longer a boy,—
you've cured me of that. Hang it, that's why I love
you! Don't you see? Ah, Gertrude!"—and his
voice fell,—"you're a great enchantress! You have
no arts, you have no beauty even, (can't a lover
deal with facts now?), but you are an enchantress
without them. It's your nature. You are so di-
vinely, damnably honest! That excellent speech just
now was meant to smother my passion; but it has
only inflamed it. You will say it was nothing but
common sense. Very likely; but that is the very
point. Your common sense captivates me. It's for
that that I love you."

He spoke with so relentless a calmness that Gertrude was sickened. Here she found herself weaker than he, while the happiness of both of them demanded that she should be stronger.

"Richard Clare," she said, "you are unkind!" There was a tremor in her voice as she spoke; and as she ceased speaking, she burst into tears. A selfish sense of victory invaded the young man's breast. He threw his arm about her; but she shook it off. "You are a coward, sir!" she cried.

"Oho!" said Richard, flushing angrily.

"You go too far; you persist beyond decency."

"You hate me now, I suppose," said Richard, brutally, like one at bay.

Gertrude brushed away her tears. "No, indeed," she answered, sending him a dry, clear glance. "To hate you, I should have to have loved you. I pity you still."

Richard looked at her a moment. "I don't feel tempted to return the feeling, Gertrude," said he. "A woman with so much head as you needs no pity."

"I have not head enough to read your sarcasm, sir; but I have heart enough to excuse it, and I mean to keep a good heart to the end. I mean to keep my temper, I mean to be just, I mean to be conclusive, and not to have to return to this matter. It's not for my pleasure, I would have you know, that I am so explicit. I have nerves as well as you.

Listen, then. If I don't love you, Richard, in your way, I don't; and if I can't, I can't. We can't love by will. But with friendship, when it is once established, I believe the will and the reason may have a great deal to do. I will, therefore, put the whole of my mind into my friendship for you, and in that way we shall perhaps be even. Such a feeling—as I shall naturally show it—will, after all, not be very different from that other feeling you ask—as I should naturally show it. Bravely to reconcile himself to such difference as there is, is no more than a man of honor ought to do. Do you understand me?"

"You have an admirable way of putting things. 'After all,' and 'such difference as there is'! The difference is the difference of marriage and no-marriage. I suppose you don't mean that you are willing to live with me without that ceremony?"

"You suppose correctly."

"Then why do you falsify matters? A woman is either a man's wife, or she isn't."

"Yes; and a woman is either a man's friend, or she isn't."

"And you are mine, and I'm an ungrateful brute not to rest satisfied! That's what you mean. Heaven knows you're right,"—and he paused a moment, with his eyes on the ground. "Don't despise me, Gertrude," he resumed. "I'm not so ungrateful as I seem. I'm very much obliged to you for the pains you have taken. Of course, I understand your not loving me. You'd be a grand fool if you did; and you're no fool, Gertrude."

"No, I'm no fool, Richard. It's a great responsibility,—it's dreadfully vulgar; but, on the whole, I'm rather glad."

"So am I. I could hate you for it; but there is no doubt it's why I love you. If you were a fool, you might love me; but I shouldn't love you, and if I must choose, I prefer that."

"Heaven has chosen for us. Ah, Richard," pursued Gertrude, with admirable simplicity, "let us be good and obey Heaven, and we shall be sure to be happy,"—and she held out her hand once more.

Richard took it and raised it to his lips. She felt their pressure and withdrew it.

"Now you must leave me," she said. "Did you ride?"

"My horse is at the village."

"You can go by the river, then. Good night."

"Good night."

The young man moved away in the gathering dusk, and Miss Whittaker stood for a moment looking after him.

To appreciate the importance of this conversation, the reader must know that Miss Gertrude Whittaker was a young woman of four-and-twenty, whose

father, recently deceased, had left her alone in the
world, with a great fortune, accumulated by various
enterprises in that part of the State. He had appointed a distant and elderly kinswoman, by name
Miss Pendexter, as his daughter's household companion; and an old friend of his own, known to
combine shrewdness with integrity, as her financial
adviser. Motherless, country-bred, and homely-
featured, Gertrude, on arriving at maturity, had
neither the tastes nor the manners of a fine lady.
Of a robust and active make, with a warm heart, a
cool head, and a very pretty talent for affairs, she
was, in virtue both of her wealth and of her tact,
one of the chief figures of the neighborhood. These
facts had forced her into a prominence which she
made no attempt to elude, and in which she now felt
thoroughly at home. She knew herself to be a
power in the land; she knew that, present and absent, she was continually talked about as the rich
Miss Whittaker; and although as modest as a woman need be, she was neither so timid nor so nervous
as to wish to compromise with her inevitable distinctions. Her feelings were, indeed, throughout,
strong, rather than delicate; and yet there was in her
whole nature, as the world had learned to look at it,
a moderation, a temperance, a benevolence, an or-
derly freedom, which bespoke universal respect.
She was impulsive, and yet discreet; economical,

and yet generous; humorous, and yet serious; keenly discerning of human distinctions, and yet almost indiscriminately hospitable; with a prodigious fund of common sense beneath all; and yet beyond this,— like the priest behind the king,—and despite her broadly prosaic, and as it were secular tone, a certain latent suggestion of heroic possibilities, which he who had once become sensible of it (supposing him to be young and enthusiastic) would linger about her hoping to detect, as you might stand watchful of a florid and vigorous dahlia, which for an instant, in your passage, should have proved deliciously fragrant. It is upon the actual existence, in more minds than one, of a mystifying sense of this sweet and remote perfume, that our story is based.

Richard Clare and Miss Whittaker were old friends. They had in the first place gone democratically to the town school together as children; and then their divergent growth, as boy and girl, had acknowledged an elastic bond in a continued intimacy between Gertrude and Fanny Clare, Richard's sister, who, however, in the fulness of time had married, and had followed her husband to California. With her departure the old relations of habit between her brother and her friend had slackened, and gradually ceased. Richard had grown up a rebellious and troublesome boy, with a disposition combining stolid apathy and hot-headed impatience in equal proportions. Losing both of his parents before he was well out of his boyhood, he had found himself at the age of sixteen in possession actual, and as he supposed uncontested, of the paternal farm. It was not long, however, before those turned up who were disposed to question his immediate ability to manage it; the result of which was, that the farm was leased for five years, and that Richard was almost forcibly abducted by a maternal uncle, living on a farm of his own some three hundred miles away. Here our young man spent the remainder of his minority, ostensibly learning agriculture with his cousins, but actually learning nothing. He had very soon established, and had subsequently enjoyed without a day's interval, the reputation of an ill-natured fool. He was dull, disobliging, brooding, lowering. Reading and shooting he liked a little, because they were solitary pastimes; but to common duties and pleasures he proved himself as incompetent as he was averse. It was possible to live with him only because he was at once too selfish and too simple for mischief. As soon as he came of age he resumed possession of the acres on which his boyhood had been passed, and toward which he gravitated under an instinct of mere local affection, rather than from any intelligent purpose. He avoided his neighbors, his father's former associates; he rejected, nay, he violated, their counsel; he informed them that he wanted no help but what he paid for, and that he expected to work his farm for himself and by himself. In short, he proved himself to their satisfaction egregiously ungrateful, conceited, and arrogant. They were not slow to discover that his incapacity was as great as his conceit. In two years he had more than undone the work of the late lessee, which had been an improvement on that of the original owner. In the third year, it seemed to those who observed him that there was something so wanton in his errors as almost to impugn his sanity. He appeared to have accepted them himself, and to have given up all pretence of work. He went about silent and sullen, like a man who feels that he has a quarrel with fate. About this time it became generally known that he was often the worse for liquor; and he hereupon acquired the deplorable reputation of a man worse than unsociable,—a man who drinks alone,—although it was still doubtful whether this practice was the cause or the effect of his poor crops. About this time, too, he resumed acquaintance with Gertrude Whittaker. For many months after his return he had been held at his distance, together with most of his rural compeers, by the knowledge of her father's bitter hostility to all possible suitors and fortune-hunters; and then, subsequently, by the illness preceding the old man's death; but when at last, on the expiration of her term of mourning, Miss Whittaker had opened to society her long blockaded ports, Richard had, to all the world's amazement, been among the first to profit by this extension of the general privilege, and to cast anchor in the wide and peaceful waters of her friendship. He found himself at this moment, considerably to his surprise, in his twenty-fourth year, that is, a few months Gertrude's junior.

It was impossible that she should not have gathered from mere juxtaposition a vague impression of his evil repute and of his peculiar relation to his neighbors, and to his own affairs. Thanks to this impression, Richard found a very warm welcome,— the welcome of compassion. Gertrude gave him a heavy arrear of news from his sister Fanny, with whom he had dropped correspondence, and, impelled by Fanny's complaints of his long silence, ventured upon a friendly admonition that he should go straight home and write a letter to California. Richard sat before her, gazing at her out of his dark eyes, and not only attempting no defence of his conduct, but rejoicing dumbly in the utter absence of any possible defence, as of an interruption to his companion's virtue. He wished that he might incontinently lay bare all his shortcomings to her delicious reproof. He carried away an extraordinary sense of general alleviation; and forthwith began a series of visits, which in the space of some ten weeks culminated in the interview with which our narrative opens. Painfully diffident in the company of most women, Richard had not from the first known what it was to be shy with Gertrude. As a man of the world finds it useful to refresh his social energies by an occasional *tête-à-tête* of an hour with himself, so Richard, with whom solitude was the rule, derived a certain austere satisfaction from an hour's contact with Miss Whittaker's consoling good sense, her abundance, her decent duties and comforts. Gradually, however, from a salutary process, this became almost an æsthetic one. It was now pleasant to go to Gertrude, because he enjoyed the contagion of her own repose, —because he witnessed her happiness without a sensation of envy,—because he forgot his own entanglements and errors,—because, finally, his soul slept away its troubles beneath her varying glance, very much as his body had often slept away its weariness in the shade of a changing willow. But the soul, like the body, will not sleep long without dreaming; and it will not dream often without wishing at last to tell its dreams. Richard had one day ventured to impart his visions to Gertrude, and the revelation had apparently given her serious pain. The fact that Richard Clare (of all men in the world!) had somehow worked himself into an intimacy with Miss

Whittaker very soon became public property among their neighbors; and in the hands of these good people, naturally enough, received an important addition in the inference that he was going to marry her. He was, of course, esteemed a very lucky fellow, and the prevalence of this impression was doubtless not without its effect on the forbearance of certain long-suffering creditors. And even if she was not to marry him, it was further argued, she yet might lend him money; for it was assumed without question that the necessity of raising money was the mainspring of Richard's suit. It is needless to inform the reader that this assumption was—to use a homely metaphor—without a leg to stand upon. Our hero had faults enough, but to be mercenary was not one of them; nor was an excessive concern on the subject of his debts one of his virtues. As for Gertrude, wherever else her perception of her friend's feelings may have been at fault, it was not at fault on this point. That he loved her as desperately as he declared, she indeed doubted; but it never occurred to her to question the purity of his affection. And so, on the other hand, it was strictly out of her heart's indifference that she rejected him, and not for the disparity of their fortunes. In accepting his very simple and natural overtures to friendship, in calling him "Richard" in remembrance of old days, and in submitting generally to the terms of their old relations, she had foreseen no sentimental catastrophe. She had viewed her friend from the first as an object of lively material concern. She had espoused his interests (like all good women, Gertrude was ever more or less of a partisan) because she loved his sister, and because she pitied himself. She would stand to him *in loco sororis*. The reader has seen that she had given herself a long day's work.

It is not to be supposed that Richard's sober retreat at the close of the walk by the river implied any instinct of resignation to the prospects which Gertrude had opened to him. It is explained rather by an intensity of purpose so deep as to fancy that it can dispense with bravado. This was not the end of his suit, but the beginning. He would not give in until he was positively beaten. It was all very well, he reflected, that Gertrude should reject him. Such a woman as she ought properly to be striven for, and there was something ridiculous in the idea that she should be easily won, whether by himself or by another. Richard was a slow thinker, but he thought more wisely than he talked; and he now took back all his angry boasts of accomplished self-mastery, and humbly surveyed the facts of the case. He was on the way to recovery, but he was by no means cured, and yet his very humility assured him that he was curable. He was no hero, but he was better than his life; he was no scholar, but in his own view at least he was no fool. He was good enough to be better; he was good enough not to sit by the hour soaking his slender brains in whiskey. And at the very least, if he was not worthy to possess Gertrude, he was yet worthy to strive to obtain her, and to live forevermore upon the glory of having been formally refused by the great Miss Whittaker. He would raise himself then to that level from which he could address her as an equal, from which he could borrow that authority of which he was now so shamefully bare. How he would do this, he was at a loss to determine. He was conscious of an immense fund of brute volition, but he cursed his barbarous ignorance, as he searched in vain for those high opposing forces the defeat of which might lend dignity to his struggle. He longed vaguely for some continuous muscular effort, at the end of which he should find himself face to face with his mistress. But as, instead of being a Pagan hero, with an enticing task-list of impossibilities, he was a plain New England farmer, with a bad conscience, and nature with him and not against him,—as, after slaying his dragon, after breaking with liquor, his work was a simple operation in common sense,—in view of these facts he found but little inspiration in his prospect. Nevertheless he fronted it bravely. He was not to obtain Gertrude by making a fortune, but by making himself a man, by learning to think. But as to learn to think is to learn to work, he would find some use for his muscle. He would keep sober and clear-headed; he would retrieve his land and pay his debts. Then let her refuse him if she could,—or if she dared, he was wont occasionally to add.

Meanwhile Gertrude on her side sat quietly at home, revolving in her own fashion a dozen ideal schemes for her friend's redemption and for the diversion of his enthusiasm. Not but what she meant rigorously to fulfil her part of the engagement to which she had invited him in that painful scene by the river. Yet whatever of that firmness, patience, and courtesy of which she possessed so large a stock she might still oppose to his importunities, she could not feel secure against repeated intrusion (for it was by this term that she was disposed to qualify all unsanctioned transgression of those final and immovable limits which she had set to her immense hospitality) without the knowledge of a partial change at least in Richard's own attitude. Such a change could only be effected through some preparatory change in his life; and a change in his life could be brought about only by the introduction of some new influence. This influence, however, was very hard to find. However positively Gertrude had dwelt upon the practical virtue of her own friendship, she was now on further reflection led sadly to distrust the exclusive use of this instrument. He was welcome enough to that, but he needed something more. It suddenly occurred to her, one morning after Richard's image had been crossing and recrossing her mental vision for a couple of hours with wearisome pertinacity, that a world of good might accrue to him through the friendship of a person so unexceptionable as Captain Severn. There was no one, she declared within herself, who would not be better for knowing such a man. She would recommend Richard to his kindness, and him she would recommend to Richard's—what? Here was the rub! Where was there common ground between Richard and such a one as he? To request him to like Richard was easy; to ask Richard to like him was ridiculous. If Richard could only know him, the work were done; he couldn't choose but love him as a brother. But to bespeak Richard's respect for an object was to fill him straightway with aversion for it. Her young friend was so pitiable a creature himself, that it had never occurred to her to appeal to his sentiments of compassion. All the world seemed above him, and he was consequently at odds with all the world. If some worthy being could be found, even less favored of nature and of fortune than himself, to such a one he might become attached by a useful sympathy. There was indeed nothing particularly enviable in Captain Severn's lot, and herein Richard might properly experience a fellow-feeling for him; but nevertheless he was apparently quite contented with it, and thus he was raised several degrees above Richard, who would be certain to find something aggressive in his equanimity. Still, for all this, Gertrude would bring them together. She had a high estimate of the Captain's generosity, and if Richard should wantonly fail to conform to the situation, the loss would be his own. It may be thought that in this enterprise Captain Severn was somewhat inconsiderately handled. But a generous woman will freely make a missionary of the man she loves. These words suggest the propriety of a short description of the person to whom they refer.

Edmund Severn was a man of eight-and-twenty, who, having for some time combated fortune and his own inclinations as a mathematical tutor in a second-rate country college, had, on the opening of the war, transferred his valor to a more heroic field. His regiment of volunteers, now at work before Richmond, had been raised in Miss Whittaker's district, and beneath her substantial encouragement. His soldiership, like his scholarship, was solid rather than brilliant. He was not destined to be heard of at home, nor to leave his regiment; but on many an important occasion in Virginia he had proved him-

self in a modest way an excellently useful man.
Coming up early in the war with a severe wound,
to be nursed by a married sister domiciled in Gertrude's neighborhood, he was, like all his fellow-
sufferers within a wide circuit, very soon honored
with a visit of anxious inquiry from Miss Whittaker,
who was as yet known to him only by report, and
who transmitted to him the warmest assurances of
sympathy and interest, together with the liveliest
offers of assistance; and, incidentally as it were to
these, a copious selection from the products of her
hot-house and store-room. Severn had taken the
air for the first time in Gertrude's own great cushioned barouche, which she had sent to his door at
an early stage of his convalescence, and which of
course he had immediately made use of to pay his
respects to his benefactress. He was confounded by
the real humility with which, on this occasion, betwixt smiles and tears, she assured him that to be of
service to such as him was for her a sacred privilege.
Never, thought the Captain as he drove away, had
he seen so much rustic breadth combined with so
much womanly grace. Half a dozen visits during
the ensuing month more than sufficed to convert him
into what is called an admirer; but, as the weeks
passed by, he felt that there were great obstacles to
his ever ripening into a lover. Captain Severn was
a serious man; he was conscientious, discreet, delib-

erate, unused to act without a definite purpose.
Whatever might be the intermediate steps, it was
necessary that the goal of an enterprise should have
become an old story to him before he took the first
steps. And, moreover, if the goal seemed a profitable or an honorable station, he was proof against
the perils or the discomforts of the journey; while
if, on the other hand, it offered no permanent repose,
he generally found but little difficulty in resisting the
incidental allurements. In pursuance of this habit,
or rather in obedience to this principle, of carefully
fixing his programme, he had asked himself whether
he was prepared to face the logical results of a series
of personal attentions to our heroine. Since he had
determined a twelvemonth before not to marry until,
by some means or another, he should have evoked a
sufficient income, no great change had taken place
in his fortunes. He was still a poor man and an
unsettled one; he was still awaiting his real vocation.
Moreover, while subject to the chances of war, he
doubted his right to engage a woman's affections:
he shrank in horror from the thought of making a
widow. Miss Whittaker was one in five thousand.
Before the luminous fact of her existence, his dim
ideal of the desirable wife had faded into vapor.
But should he allow this fact to invalidate all the
stern precepts of his reason? He could no more
afford to marry a rich woman than a poor one.

When he should have earned a subsistence for two, then he would be free to marry whomsoever he might fancy,—a beggar or an heiress. The truth is, that the Captain was a great deal too proud. It was his fault that he could not bring himself to forget the difference between his poverty and Gertrude's wealth. He would of course have resented the insinuation that the superior fortune of the woman he loved should really have force to prevent him from declaring his love; but there is no doubt that in the case before us this fact arrested his passion in its origin. Severn had a most stoical aversion to being in debt. It is certain that, after all, he would have made a very graceful debtor to his mistress or his wife; but while a woman was as yet neither his mistress nor his wife, the idea of being beholden to her was essentially distasteful to him. It would have been a question with one who knew him, whether at this juncture this frigid instinct was destined to resist the warmth of Gertrude's charms, or whether it was destined gradually to melt away. There would have been no question, however, but that it could maintain itself only at the cost of great suffering to its possessor. At this moment, then, Severn had made up his mind that Gertrude was not for him, and that it behooved him to be sternly vigilant both of his impulses and his impressions. That Miss Whittaker, with a hundred rational cares, was anything less than supremely oblivious of him, individually, it never occurred to him to suspect. The truth is, that Gertrude's private and personal emotions were entertained in a chamber of her heart so remote from the portals of speech that no sound of their revelry found its way into the world. She constantly thought of her modest, soldierly, scholarly friend as of one whom a wise woman might find it very natural to love. But what was she to him? A local roadside figure,—at the very most a sort of millionaire Maud Muller,—with whom it was pleasant for a lonely wayfarer to exchange a friendly "good-morning." Her duty was to fold her arms resignedly, to sit quietly on the sofa, and watch a great happiness sink below the horizon. With this impression on Gertrude's part it is not surprising that Severn was not wrenched out of himself. The prodigy was apparently to be wrought—if wrought at all—by her common, unbought sweetness. It is true that this was of a potency sufficient almost to work prodigies; but as yet its effect upon Severn had been none other than its effect upon all the world. It kept him in his kindliest humor. It kept him even in the humor of talking sentiment; but although, in the broad sunshine of her listening, his talk bloomed thick with field-flowers, he never invited her to pluck the least little daisy. It was with perfect honesty, therefore, that she had rebutted Richard's insinuation that the Captain enjoyed any especial favor. He was as yet but another of the pensioners of her good-nature.

The result of Gertrude's meditations was, that she despatched a note to each of her two friends, requesting them to take tea with her on the following day. A couple of hours before tea-time she received a visit from one Major Luttrel, who was recruiting for a United States regiment at a large town, some ten miles away, and who had ridden over in the afternoon, in accordance with a general invitation conveyed to him through an old lady who had bespoken Miss Whittaker's courtesy for him as a man of delightful manners and wonderful talents. Gertrude, on her venerable friend's representations, had replied, with her wonted alacrity, that she would be very glad to see Major Luttrel, should he ever come that way, and then had thought no more about him until his card was brought to her as she was dressing for the evening. He found so much to say to her, that the interval passed very rapidly for both of them before the simultaneous entrance of Miss Pendexter and of Gertrude's guests. The two officers were already slightly known to each other, and Richard was accordingly presented to each of them. They eyed the distracted-looking young farmer with some curiosity. Richard's was at all times a figure to attract attention; but now he was almost picturesque (so Severn thought at least) with his careless garments, his pale face, his dark mistrustful eyes, and his nervous movements. Major Luttrel, who struck Gertrude as at once very agreeable and the least bit in the world disagreeable, was, of course, invited to remain,—which he straightway consented to do; and it soon became evident to Miss Whittaker that her little scheme was destined to miscarry. Richard practised a certain defiant silence, which, as she feared, gave him eventually a decidedly ridiculous air. His companions displayed toward their hostess that half-avowed effort to shine and to outshine natural to clever men who find themselves concurring to the entertainment of a young and agreeable woman. Richard sat by, wondering, in splenetic amazement, whether he was an ignorant boor, or whether they were only a brace of inflated snobs. He decided, correctly enough, in substance, for the former hypothesis. For it seemed to him that Gertrude's consummate accommodation (for as such he viewed it) of her tone and her manner to theirs added prodigiously (so his lover's instinct taught him) to her loveliness and dignity. How magnanimous an impulse on Richard's part was this submission for his sweetheart's sake to a fact damning to his own vanity, could have been determined only by one who knew the proportions of that vanity. He writhed and chafed under the polish of tone and the

variety of allusion by which the two officers consigned him to insignificance; but he was soon lost
in wonder at the mettlesome grace and vivacity with
which Gertrude sustained her share of the conversation. For a moment it seemed to him that her
tenderness for his equanimity (for should she not
know his mind,—she who had made it?) might
reasonably have caused her to forego such an exhibition of her social accomplishments as would but
remind him afresh of his own deficiencies; but the
next moment he asked himself, with a great revul-
sion of feeling, whether he, a conscious suitor, should
fear to know his mistress in her integrity. As he
gulped down the sickening fact of his comparative,
nay, his absolute ignorance of the great world represented by his rivals, he felt like anticipating its
consequences by a desperate sally into the very field
of their conversation. To some such movement
Gertrude was continually inviting him by her glances,
her smiles, her questions, and her appealing silence.
But poor Richard knew that, if he should attempt
to talk, he would choke; and this assurance he imparted to his friend in a look piteously eloquent.
He was conscious of a sensation of rage under which
his heart was fast turning into a fiery furnace,
destined to consume all his good resolutions. He
could not answer for the future now. Suddenly, as
tea was drawing to a close, he became aware that

Captain Severn had lapsed into a silence very nearly as profound as his own, and that he was covertly watching the progress of a lively dialogue between Miss Whittaker and Major Luttrel. He had the singular experience of seeing his own feelings reflected in the Captain's face; that is, he discerned there an incipient jealousy. Severn too was in love!

On rising from table, Gertrude proposed an adjournment to the garden, where she was very fond of entertaining her friends at this hour. The sun had sunk behind a long line of hills, far beyond the opposite bank of the river, a portion of which was discernible through a gap in the intervening wood. The high-piled roof and chimney-stacks, the picturesquely crowded surface, of the old patched and renovated farm-house which served Gertrude as a villa, were ruddy with the declining rays. Our friends' long shadows were thrown over the short grass. Gertrude, having graciously anticipated the gentlemen's longing for their cigars, suggested a stroll toward the river. Before she knew it, she had accepted Major Luttrel's arm; and as Miss Pendexter preferred remaining at home, Severn and Richard found themselves lounging side by side at a short distance behind their hostess. Gertrude, who had marked the reserve which had suddenly fallen upon Captain Severn, and in her simplicity had referred it to some unwitting failure of attention on her own part, had hoped to repair her neglect by having him at her own side. She was in some degree consoled, however, by the sight of his happy juxtaposition with Richard. As for Richard, now that he was on his feet and in the open air, he found it easier to speak.

"Who is that man?" he asked, nodding toward the Major.

"Major Luttrel, of the —th Artillery."

"I don't like his face much," said Richard.

"Don't you?" rejoined Severn, amused at his companion's bluntness. "He's not handsome, but he looks like a soldier."

"He looks like a rascal, I think," said Richard.

Severn laughed outright, so that Gertrude glanced back at him. "Dear me! I think you put it rather strongly. I should call it a very intelligent face."

Richard was sorely perplexed. He had expected to find acceptance for his bitterest animadversions, and lo! here was the Captain fighting for his enemy. Such a man as that was no rival. So poor a hater could be but a poor lover. Nevertheless, a certain new-born mistrust of his old fashion of measuring human motives prevented him from adopting this conclusion as final. He would try another question.

"Do you know Miss Whittaker well?" he asked.

"Tolerably well. She was very kind to me when

I was ill.   Since then I've seen her some dozen times."

"That's a way she has, being kind," said Richard, with what he deemed considerable shrewdness.   But as the Captain merely puffed his cigar responsively, he pursued, "What do you think of her face?"

"I like it very much," said the Captain.

"She isn't beautiful," said Richard, cunningly.

Severn was silent a moment, and then, just as Richard was about to dismiss him from his thoughts, as neither formidable nor satisfactory, he replied, with some emphasis, "You mean she isn't pretty. She *is* beautiful, I think, in spite of the irregularity of her face.   It's a face not to be forgotten.   She has no features, no color, no lilies or roses, no attitudes; but she has *looks,* expression.   Her face has *character;* and so has her figure.   It has no 'style,' as they call it; but that only belongs properly to a work of art, which Miss Whittaker's figure isn't, thank Heaven!   She's as unconscious of it as Nature herself."

Severn spoke Richard's mind as well as his own. That "She isn't beautiful" had been an extempore version of the young man's most sacred dogma, namely, She is beautiful.   The reader will remember that he had so translated it on a former occasion. Now, all that he felt was a sense of gratitude to the Captain for having put it so much more finely

than he, the above being his choicest public expression of it. But the Captain's eyes, somewhat brightened by his short but fervid speech, were following
Gertrude's slow steps. Richard saw that he could
learn more from them than from any further oral
declaration; for something in the mouth beneath
them seemed to indicate that it had judged itself to
have said enough, and it was obviously not the mouth
of a simpleton. As he thus deferred with an un-
wonted courtesy to the Captain's silence, and transferred his gaze sympathetically to Gertrude's
shapely shoulders and to her listening ear, he gave
utterance to a telltale sigh,—a sigh which there was
no mistaking. Severn looked about; it was now his
turn to scrutinize. "Good Heavens!" he exclaimed,
"that boy is in love with her!"

After the first shock of surprise, he accepted this
fact with rational calmness. Why shouldn't he be
in love with her? *"Je le suis bien,"* said the Captain;
"or, rather, I'm not." Could it be, Severn pursued,
that he was a favorite? He was a mannerless young
farmer; but it was plain that he had a soul of his
own. He almost wished, indeed, that Richard might
prove to be in Gertrude's good graces. "But if he
is," he reflected, "why should he sigh? It is true
that there is no arguing for lovers. I, who am out
in the cold, take my comfort in whistling most im-
pertinently. It may be that my friend here groans

for very bliss. I confess, however, that he scarcely looks like a favored swain."

And forthwith this faint-hearted gentleman felt a twinge of pity for Richard's obvious infelicity; and as he compared it with the elaborately defensive condition of his own affections, he felt a further pang of self-contempt. But it was easier to restore the equilibrium of his self-respect by an immediate cession of the field, than by contesting it against this wofully wounded knight. "Whether he wins her or not, he'll fight for her," the Captain declared; and as he glanced at Major Luttrel, he felt that this was a sweet assurance. He had conceived a singular distrust of the Major.

They had now reached the water's edge, where Gertrude, having arrested her companion, had turned about, expectant of her other guests. As they came up, Severn saw, or thought that he saw (which is a very different thing), that her first look was at Richard. The "admirer" in his breast rose fratricidal for a moment against the quiet observer; but the next, it was pinioned again. "Amen," said the Captain; "it's none of my business."

At this moment, Richard was soaring most heroically. The end of his anguish had been a sudden intoxication. He surveyed the scene before him with a kindling fancy. Why should he stand tongue-tied in sullen mistrust of fortune, when all nature beckoned him into the field? There was the river-path where, a fortnight before, he had found an eloquence attested by Gertrude's tears. There was sweet Gertrude herself, whose hand he had kissed and whose waist he had clasped. Surely, he was master here! Before he knew it, he had begun to talk,—rapidly, nervously, and almost defiantly. Major Luttrel, having made an observation about the prettiness of the river, Richard entered upon a description of its general course and its superior beauty upon his own place, together with an enumeration of the fish which were to be found in it, and a story about a great overflow ten years before. He spoke in fair, coherent terms, but with singular intensity and vehemence, and with his head thrown back and his eyes on the opposite bank. At last he stopped, feeling that he had given proof of his manhood, and looked towards Gertrude, whose eyes he had been afraid to meet until he had seen his adventure to a close. But she was looking at Captain Severn, under the impression that Richard had secured his auditor. Severn was looking at Luttrel, and Luttrel at Miss Whittaker; and all were apparently so deep in observation that they had marked neither his speech nor his silence. "Truly," thought the young man, "I'm well out of the circle!" But he was resolved to be patient still, which was assuredly, all things considered, a very brave resolve.

Yet there was always something spasmodic and unnatural in Richard's magnanimity. A touch in the wrong place would cause it to collapse. It was Gertrude's evil fortune to administer this touch at present. As the party turned about toward the house, Richard stepped to her side and offered her his arm, hoping in his heart—so implicitly did he count upon her sympathy, so almost boyishly, filially, did he depend upon it—for some covert token that his heroism, such as it was, had not been lost upon her.

But Gertrude, intensely preoccupied by the desire to repair her fancied injustice to the Captain, shook her head at him without even meeting his eye. "Thank you," she said; "I want Captain Severn," who forthwith approached.

Poor Richard felt his feet touch the ground again. He felt that he could have flung the Captain into the stream. Major Luttrel placed himself at Gertrude's other elbow, and Richard stood behind them, almost livid with spite, and half resolved to turn upon his heel and make his way home by the river. But it occurred to him that a more elaborate vengeance would be to follow the trio before him back to the lawn, and there make it a silent and scathing bow. Accordingly, when they reached the house, he stood aloof and bade Gertrude a grim good-night. He trembled with eagerness to see whether she would make an attempt to detain him. But Miss Whittaker, reading in his voice—it had grown too dark to see his face at the distance at which he stood —the story of some fancied affront, and unconsciously contrasting it, perhaps, with Severn's clear and unwarped accents, obeyed what she deemed a prompting of self-respect, and gave him, without her hand, a farewell as cold as his own. It is but fair to add, that, a couple of hours later, as she reviewed the incidents of the evening, she repented most generously of this little act of justice.

PART II

RICHARD got through the following week he hardly knew how. He found occupation, to a much greater extent than he was actually aware of, in a sordid and yet heroic struggle with himself. For several months now, he had been leading, under Gertrude's inspiration, a strictly decent and sober life. So long as he was at comparative peace with Gertrude and with himself, such a life was more than easy; it was delightful. It produced a moral buoyancy infinitely more delicate and more constant than the gross exhilaration of his old habits. There was a kind of fascination in adding hour to hour, and day to day, in this record of his new-born austerity. Having abjured excesses, he practised temperance after the fashion of a novice: he raised it (or reduced it) to abstinence. He was like an unclean man who, having washed himself clean, remains in the water for the love of it. He wished to be religiously, superstitiously pure. This was easy, as we have said, so long as his goddess smiled, even though it were as a goddess indeed,—as a creature unattainable. But when she frowned, and the heavens grew dark, Richard's sole dependence was in his own will,—as flimsy a trust for an upward scramble, one would have premised, as a tuft of grass on the face of a perpendicular cliff. Flimsy as it looked, however, it served him. It started and crumbled, but it held, if only by a single fibre. When Richard had cantered fifty yards away from Gertrude's gate in a fit of stupid rage, he suddenly pulled up his horse and gulped down his passion, and swore an oath, that, suffer what torments of feeling he might, he would not at least break the continuity of his gross physical soberness. It was enough to be drunk in mind; he would not be drunk in body. A singular, almost ridiculous feeling of antagonism to Gertrude lent force to this resolution. "No, madam," he cried within himself, "I shall *not* fall back. Do your best! I shall keep straight." We often outweather great offences and afflictions through a certain healthy instinct of egotism. Richard went to bed that night as grim and sober as a Trappist monk; and his foremost impulse the next day was to plunge headlong into some physical labor which should not allow him a moment's interval of idleness. He found no labor to his taste; but he

spent the day so actively, in the mechanical anni-
hilation of the successive hours, that Gertrude's
image found no chance squarely to face him.　He
was engaged in the work of self-preservation,—the
most serious and absorbing work possible to man.
Compared to the results here at stake, his passion
for Gertrude seemed but a fiction.　It is perhaps
difficult to give a more lively impression of the
vigor of this passion, of its maturity and its strength,
than by simply stating that it discreetly held itself
in abeyance until Richard had set at rest his doubts
of that which lies nearer than all else to the heart
of man,—his doubts of the strength of his will.　He
answered these doubts by subjecting his resolution
to a course of such cruel temptations as were likely
either to shiver it to a myriad of pieces, or to season
it perfectly to all the possible requirements of life.
He took long rides over the country, passing within
a stone's throw of as many of the scattered wayside
taverns as could be combined in a single circuit.
As he drew near them he sometimes slackened his
pace, as if he were about to dismount, pulled up his
horse, gazed a moment, then, thrusting in his spurs,
galloped away again like one pursued.　At other
times, in the late evening, when the window-panes
were aglow with the ruddy light within, he would
walk slowly by, looking at the stars, and, after
maintaining this stoical pace for a couple of miles,

would hurry home to his own lonely and black-windowed dwelling. Having successfully performed this feat a certain number of times, he found his love coming back to him, bereft in the interval of its attendant jealousy. In obedience to it, he one morning leaped upon his horse and repaired to Gertrude's abode, with no definite notion of the terms in which he should introduce himself.

He had made himself comparatively sure of his will; but he was yet to acquire the mastery of his impulses. As he gave up his horse, according to his wont, to one of the men at the stable, he saw another steed stalled there which he recognized as Captain Severn's. "Steady, my boy," he murmured to himself, as he would have done to a frightened horse. On his way across the broad court-yard toward the house, he encountered the Captain, who had just taken his leave. Richard gave him a generous salute (he could not trust himself to more), and Severn answered with what was at least a strictly just one. Richard observed, however, that he was very pale, and that he was pulling a rosebud to pieces as he walked; whereupon our young man quickened his step. Finding the parlor empty, he instinctively crossed over to a small room adjoining it, which Gertrude had converted into a modest conservatory; and as he did so, hardly knowing it, he lightened his heavy-shod tread. The glass door was open and

Richard looked in. There stood Gertrude with her back to him, bending apart with her hands a couple of tall flowering plants, and looking through the glazed partition behind them. Advancing a step, and glancing over the young girl's shoulder, Richard had just time to see Severn mounting his horse at the stable door, before Gertrude, startled by his approach, turned hastily round. Her face was flushed hot, and her eyes brimming with tears.

"You!" she exclaimed, sharply.

Richard's head swam. That single word was so charged with cordial impatience that it seemed the death-knell of his hope. He stepped inside the room and closed the door, keeping his hand on the knob.

"Gertrude," he said, "you love that man!"

"Well, sir?"

"Do you confess it?" cried Richard.

"Confess it? Richard Clare, how dare you use such language? I'm in no humor for a scene. Let me pass."

Gertrude was angry; but as for Richard, it may almost be said that he was mad. "One scene a day is enough, I suppose," he cried. "What are these tears about? Wouldn't he have you? Did he refuse you, as you refused me? Poor Gertrude!"

Gertrude looked at him a moment with concentrated scorn. "You fool!" she said, for all answer.

She pushed his hand from the latch, flung open the door, and moved rapidly away.

Left alone, Richard sank down on a sofa and covered his face with his hands. It burned them, but he sat motionless, repeating to himself, mechanically, as if to avert thought, "You fool! you fool!" At last he got up and made his way out.

It seemed to Gertrude, for several hours after this scene, that she had at this juncture a strong case against Fortune. It is not our purpose to repeat the words which she had exchanged with Captain Severn. They had come within a single step of an *éclaircissement,* and when but another movement would have flooded their souls with light, some malignant influence had seized them by the throats. Had they too much pride?—too little imagination? We must content ourselves with this hypothesis. Severn, then, had walked mechanically across the yard, saying to himself, "She belongs to another"; and adding, as he saw Richard, "and such another." Gertrude had stood at her window, repeating, under her breath, "He belongs to himself, himself alone." And as if this was not enough, when misconceived, slighted, wounded, she had faced about to her old, passionless, dutiful past, there on the path of retreat to this asylum Richard Clare had arisen to forewarn her that she should find no peace even at home. There was something in the violent impertinence of his appearance at this moment which gave her a dreadful feeling that fate was against her. More than this. There entered into her emotions a certain minute particle of awe of the man whose passion was so uncompromising. She felt that it was out of place any longer to pity him. He was the slave of his passion; but his passion was strong. In her reaction against the splendid civility of Severn's silence, (the real antithesis of which would have been simply the perfect courtesy of explicit devotion,) she found herself touching with pleasure on the fact of Richard's brutality. He at least had ventured to insult her. He had loved her enough to forget himself. He had dared to make himself odious in her eyes, because he had cast away his sanity. What cared he for the impression he made? He cared only for the impression he received. The violence of this reaction, however, was the measure of its duration. It was impossible that she should walk backward so fast without stumbling. Brought to her senses by this accident, she became aware that her judgment was missing. She smiled to herself as she reflected that it had been taking holiday for a whole afternoon. "Richard was right," she said to herself. "I am no fool. I can't be a fool if I try. I'm too thoroughly my father's daughter for that. I love that man, but I love myself better. Of course, then, I don't deserve to have him. If I loved

him in a way to merit his love, I would sit down this
moment and write him a note telling him that if
he does not come back to me, I shall die. But I
shall neither write the note nor die. I shall live and
grow stout, and look after my chickens and my
flowers and my colts, and thank the Lord in my old
age that I have never done anything unwomanly.
Well! I'm as He made me. Whether I can deceive
others, I know not; but I certainly can't deceive
myself. I'm quite as sharp as Gertrude Whittaker;
and this it is that has kept me from making a fool
of myself and writing to poor Richard the note that
I wouldn't write to Captain Severn. I needed to
fancy myself wronged. I suffer so little! I needed
a sensation! So, shrewd Yankee that I am, I thought
I would get one cheaply by taking up that unhappy
boy! Heaven preserve me from the heroics, especially the economical heroics! The one heroic course
possible, I decline. What, then, have I to complain
of? Must I tear my hair because a man of taste
has resisted my unspeakable charms? To be charming, you must be charmed yourself, or at least you
must be able to be charmed; and that apparently
I'm not. I didn't love him, or he would have known
it. Love gets love, and no-love gets none."

But at this point of her meditations Gertrude
almost broke down. She felt that she was assigning
herself but a dreary future. Never to be loved but

by such a one as Richard Clare was a cheerless prospect; for it was identical with an eternal spinsterhood. "Am I, then," she exclaimed, quite as passionately as a woman need do,—"am I, then, cut off from a woman's dearest joys? What blasphemous nonsense! One thing is plain: I am made to be a mother; the wife may take care of herself. I am made to be a wife; the mistress may take care of *her*self. I am in the Lord's hands," added the poor girl, who, whether or no she could forget herself in an earthly love, had at all events this mark of a spontaneous nature, that she could forget herself in a heavenly one. But in the midst of her pious emotion, she was unable to subdue her conscience. It smote her heavily for her meditated falsity to Richard, for her miserable readiness to succumb to the strong temptation to seek a momentary resting-place in his gaping heart. She recoiled from this thought as from an act cruel and immoral. Was Richard's heart the place for her now, any more than it had been a month before? Was she to apply for comfort where she would not apply for counsel? Was she to drown her decent sorrows and regrets in a base, a dishonest, an extemporized passion? Having done the young man so bitter a wrong in intention, nothing would appease her magnanimous remorse (as time went on) but to repair it in fact. She went so far as keenly to regret the harsh words she had cast upon him in the conservatory. He had been insolent and unmannerly; but he had an excuse. Much should be forgiven him, for he loved much. Even now that Gertrude had imposed upon her feelings a sterner regimen than ever, she could not defend herself from a sweet and sentimental thrill—a thrill in which, as we have intimated, there was something of a tremor—at the recollection of his strident accents and his angry eyes. It was yet far from her heart to desire a renewal, however brief, of this exhibition. She wished simply to efface from the young man's morbid soul the impression of a real contempt; for she knew—or she thought that she knew—that against such an impression he was capable of taking the most fatal and inconsiderate comfort.

Before many mornings had passed, accordingly, she had a horse saddled, and, dispensing with attendance, she rode rapidly over to his farm. The house door and half the windows stood open; but no answer came to her repeated summons. She made her way to the rear of the house, to the barn-yard, thinly tenanted by a few common fowl, and across the yard to a road which skirted its lower extremity and was accessible by an open gate. No human figure was in sight; nothing was visible in the hot stillness but the scattered and ripening crops, over which, in spite of her nervous solicitude, Miss Whittaker cast the glance of a connoisseur. A great uneasiness filled her mind as she measured the rich domain apparently deserted of its young master, and reflected that she perhaps was the cause of its abandonment. Ah, where was Richard? As she looked and listened in vain, her heart rose to her throat, and she felt herself on the point of calling all too wistfully upon his name. But her voice was stayed by the sound of a heavy rumble, as of cart-wheels, beyond a turn in the road. She touched up her horse and cantered along until she reached the turn. A great four-wheeled cart, laden with masses of newly broken stone, and drawn by four oxen, was slowly advancing towards her. Beside it, patiently cracking his whip and shouting monotonously, walked a young man in a slouched hat and a red shirt, with his trousers thrust into his dusty boots. It was Richard. As he saw Gertrude, he halted a moment, amazed, and then advanced, flicking the air with his whip. Gertrude's heart went out towards him in a silent Thank God! Her next reflection was that he had never looked so well. The truth is, that, in this rough adjustment, the native barbarian was duly represented. His face and neck were browned by a week in the fields, his eye was clear, his step seemed to have learned a certain manly dignity from its attendance on the heavy bestial tramp. Gertrude, as he reached her side, pulled up her horse and held out her gloved fingers to his brown dusty hand. He took them, looked for a moment into her face, and for the second time raised them to his lips.

"Excuse my glove," she said, with a little smile.

"Excuse mine," he answered, exhibiting his sunburnt, work-stained hand.

"Richard," said Gertrude, "you never had less need of excuse in your life. You never looked half so well."

He fixed his eyes upon her a moment. "Why, you have forgiven me!" he exclaimed.

"Yes," said Gertrude, "I have forgiven you,—both you and myself. We both of us behaved very absurdly, but we both of us had reason. I wish you had come back."

Richard looked about him, apparently at loss for a rejoinder. "I have been very busy," he said, at last, with a simplicity of tone slightly studied. An odd sense of dramatic effect prompted him to say neither more nor less.

An equally delicate instinct forbade Gertrude to express all the joy which this assurance gave her. Excessive joy would have implied undue surprise; and it was a part of her plan frankly to expect the best things of her companion. "If you have been busy," she said, "I congratulate you. What have you been doing?"

"O, a hundred things. I have been quarrying,

and draining, and clearing, and I don't know what all. I thought the best thing was just to put my own hands to it. I am going to make a stone fence along the great lot on the hill there. Wallace is forever grumbling about his boundaries. I'll fix them once for all. What are you laughing at?"

"I am laughing at certain foolish apprehensions that I have been indulging in for a week past. You are wiser than I, Richard. I have no imagination."

"Do you mean that *I* have? I haven't enough to guess what you *do* mean."

"Why, do you suppose, have I come over this morning?"

"Because you thought I was sulking on account of your having called me a fool."

"Sulking, or worse. What do I deserve for the wrong I have done you?"

"You have done me no wrong. You reasoned fairly enough. You are not obliged to know me better than I know myself. It's just like you to be ready to take back that bad word, and try to make yourself believe that it was unjust. But it was perfectly just, and therefore I have managed to bear it. I *was* a fool at that moment,—a stupid, impudent fool. I don't know whether that man had been making to love to you or not. But you had, I think, been feeling love for him,—you looked it; I should have been less than a man, I should be unworthy of your—your affection, if I had failed to see it. I did see it,—I saw it as clearly as I see those oxen now; and yet I bounced in with my own ill-timed claims. To do so was to be a fool. To have been other than a. fool would have been to have waited, to have backed out, to have bitten my tongue off before I spoke, to have done anything but what I did. I have no right to claim you, Gertrude, until I can woo you better than that. It was the most fortunate thing in the world that you spoke as you did; it was even kind. It saved me all the misery of groping about for a starting-point. Not to have spoken as you did would have been to fail of justice; and then, probably, I should have sulked, or, as you very considerately say, done worse. I had made a false move in the game, and the only thing to do was to repair it. But you were not obliged to know that I would so readily admit my move to have been false. Whenever I have made a fool of myself before, I have been for sticking it out, and trying to turn all mankind—that is, *you*—into a fool too, so that I shouldn't be an exception. But this time, I think, I had a kind of inspiration. I felt that my case was desperate. I felt that if I adopted my folly now I adopted it forever. The other day I met a man who had just come home from Europe, and who spent last summer in Switzerland. He was telling me about the mountain-climbing over there, —how they get over the glaciers, and all that. He said that you sometimes came upon great slippery, steep, snow-covered slopes that end short off in a precipice, and that if you stumble or lose your footing as you cross them horizontally, why you go shooting down, and you're gone; that is, but for one little dodge. You have a long walking-pole with a sharp end, you know, and as you feel yourself sliding,—it's as likely as not to be in a sitting posture, —you just take this and ram it into the snow before you, and there you are, stopped. The thing is, of course, to drive it in far enough, so that it won't yield or break; and in any case it hurts infernally to come whizzing down upon this upright pole. But the interruption gives you time to pick yourself up. Well, so it was with me the other day. I stumbled and fell; I slipped, and was whizzing downward; but I just drove in my pole and pulled up short. It nearly tore me in two; but it saved my life." Richard made this speech with one hand leaning on the neck of Gertrude's horse, and the other on his own side, and with his head slightly thrown back and his eyes on hers. She had sat quietly in her saddle, returning his gaze. He had spoken slowly and deliberately; but without hesitation and without heat. "This is not romance," thought Gertrude, "it's reality." And this feeling it was that dictated her reply, divesting it of romance so effectually as almost to make it sound trivial.

"It was fortunate you had a walking-pole," she said.

"I shall never travel without one again."

"Never, at least," smiled Gertrude, "with a companion who has the bad habit of pushing you off the path."

"Oh, you may push all you like," said Richard. "I give you leave. But isn't this enough about myself?"

"That's as you think."

"Well, it's all I have to say for the present, except that I am prodigiously glad to see you, and that of course you will stay awhile."

"But you have your work to do."

"Dear me, never you mind my work. I've earned my dinner this morning, if you have no objection: and I propose to share it with you. So we will go back to the house." He turned her horse's head about, started up his oxen with his voice, and walked along beside her on the grassy roadside, with one hand in the horse's mane, and the other swinging his whip.

Before they reached the yard-gate, Gertrude had revolved his speech. "Enough about himself," she said, silently echoing his words. "Yes, Heaven be praised, it *is* about himself. I am but a means in this matter,—he himself, his own character, his own happiness, is the end." Under this conviction it seemed to her that her part was appreciably simplified. Richard was learning wisdom and self-control, and to exercise his reason. Such was the suit that he was destined to gain. Her duty was as far as possible to remain passive, and not to interfere with the working of the gods who had selected her as the instrument of their prodigy. As they reached the gate, Richard made a trumpet of his hands, and sent a ringing summons into the fields; whereupon a farm-boy approached, and, with an undisguised stare of amazement at Gertrude, took charge of his master's team. Gertrude rode up to the door-step, where her host assisted her to dismount, and bade her go in and make herself at home, while he busied himself with the bestowal of her horse. She found that, in her absence, the old woman who administered her friend's household had reappeared, and had laid out the preparations for his mid-day meal. By the time he returned, with his face and head shining from a fresh ablution, and his shirt-sleeves decently concealed by a coat, Gertrude had apparently won the complete confidence of the good wife.

Gertrude doffed her hat, and tucked up her riding-skirt, and sat down to a *tête-à-tête* over Richard's crumpled table-cloth. The young man played the host very soberly and naturally; and Gertrude hardly knew whether to augur from his perfect self-possession that her star was already on the wane, or that it had waxed into a steadfast and eternal sun. The solution of her doubts was not far to seek; Richard was absolutely at his ease in her presence. He had told her, indeed, that she intoxicated him; and truly, in those moments when she was compelled to oppose her dewy eloquence to his fervid importunities, her whole presence seemed to him to exhale a singularly potent sweetness. He had told her that she was an enchantress, and this assertion, too, had its measure of truth. But her spell was a steady one; it sprang not from her beauty, her wit, her figure,—it sprang from her character. When she found herself aroused to appeal or to resistance, Richard's pulses were quickened to what he had called intoxication, not by her smiles, her gestures, her glances, or any accession of that material beauty which she did not possess, but by a generous sense of her virtues in action. In other words, Gertrude exercised the magnificent power of making her lover forget her face. Agreeably to this fact, his habitual feeling in her presence was one of deep repose,—a sensation not unlike that which in the early afternoon, as he lounged in his orchard with a pipe, he derived from the sight of the hot and vaporous hills. He was innocent, then, of that delicious trouble which Ger-

trude's thoughts had touched upon as a not unnatural result of her visit, and which another
woman's fancy would perhaps have dwelt upon as
an indispensable proof of its success. "Porphyro
grew faint," the poet assures us, as he stood in
Madeline's chamber on Saint Agnes' eve. But Richard did not in the least grow faint now that his
mistress was actually filling his musty old room with
her voice, her touch, her looks; that she was sitting
in his unfrequented chairs, trailing her skirt over
his faded carpet, casting her perverted image upon
his mirror, and breaking his daily bread. He was
not fluttered when he sat at her well-served table,
and trod her muffled floors. Why, then, should he
be fluttered now? Gertrude was herself in all places,
and (once granted that she was at peace) to be at
her side was to drink peace as fully in one place as
in another.

Richard accordingly ate a great working-day dinner in Gertrude's despite, and she ate a small one for
his sake. She asked questions moreover, and offered
counsel with most sisterly freedom. She deplored
the rents in his table-cloth, and the dismemberments
of his furniture; and, although by no means absurdly fastidious in the matter of household elegance, she could not but think that Richard would
be a happier and a better man if he were a little
more comfortable. She forbore, however, to criti-

cise the poverty of his *entourage,* for she felt that
the obvious answer was, that such a state of things
was the penalty of his living alone; and it was desirable, under the circumstances, that this idea
should remain implied.

When at last Gertrude began to bethink herself
of going, Richard broke a long silence by the following question: "Gertrude, *do* you love that man?"

"Richard," she answered, "I refused to tell you
before, because you asked the question as a right.
Of course you do so no longer. No. I do not love
him. I have been near it,—but I have missed it.
And now good-by."

For a week after her visit, Richard worked as
bravely and steadily as he had done before it. But
one morning he woke up lifeless, morally speaking.
His strength had suddenly left him. He had been
straining his faith in himself to a prodigious tension,
and the chord had suddenly snapped. In the hope
that Gertrude's tender fingers might repair it, he
rode over to her towards evening. On his way
through the village, he found people gathered in
knots, reading fresh copies of the Boston newspa-
pers over each other's shoulders, and learned that
tidings had just come of a great battle in Virginia,
which was also a great defeat. He procured a copy
of the paper from a man who had read it out, and
made haste to Gertrude's dwelling.

Gertrude received his story with those passionate imprecations and regrets which were then in fashion. Before long, Major Luttrel presented himself, and for half an hour there was no talk but about the battle. The talk, however, was chiefly between Gertrude and the Major, who found considerable ground for difference, she being a great radical and he a decided conservative. Richard sat by, listening apparently, but with the appearance of one to whom the matter of the discourse was of much less interest than the manner of those engaged in it. At last, when tea was announced, Gertrude told her friends, very frankly, that she would not invite them to remain,—that her heart was too heavy with her country's woes, and with the thought of so great a butchery, to allow her to play the hostess,—and that, in short, she was in the humor to be alone. Of course there was nothing for the gentlemen but to obey; but Richard went out cursing the law, under which, in the hour of his mistress' sorrow, his company was a burden and not a relief. He watched in vain, as he bade her farewell, for some little sign that she would fain have him stay, but that as she wished to get rid of his companion civility demanded that she should dismiss them both. No such sign was forthcoming, for the simple reason that Gertrude was sensible of no conflict between her desires. The men mounted their horses in silence, and rode slowly

along the lane which led from Miss Whittaker's
stables to the high-road. As they approached the
top of the lane, they perceived in the twilight a
mounted figure coming towards them. Richard's
heart began to beat with an angry foreboding, which
was confirmed as the rider drew near and disclosed
Captain Severn's features. Major Luttrel and he,
being bound in courtesy to a brief greeting, pulled
up their horses; and as an attempt to pass them in
narrow quarters would have been a greater incivility
than even Richard was prepared to commit, he likewise halted.

"This is ugly news, isn't it?" said Severn. "It
has determined me to go back to-morrow."

"Go back where?" asked Richard.

"To my regiment."

"Are you well enough?" asked Major Luttrel.
"How is that wound?"

"It's so much better that I believe it can finish getting well down there as easily as here. Good-by,
Major. I hope we shall meet again." And he shook
hands with Major Luttrel. "Good by, Mr. Clare."
And, somewhat to Richard's surprise, he stretched
over and held out his hand to him.

Richard felt that it was tremulous, and, looking
hard into his face, he thought it wore a certain un-
wonted look of excitement. And then his fancy
coursed back to Gertrude, sitting where he had left

her, in the sentimental twilight, alone with her heavy
heart. With a word, he reflected, a single little
word, a look, a motion, this happy man whose hand
I hold can heal her sorrows. "Oh!" cried Richard,
"that by this hand I might hold him fast forever!"

It seemed to the Captain that Richard's grasp was
needlessly protracted and severe. "What a grip the
poor fellow has!" he thought. "Good-by," he repeated aloud, disengaging himself.

"Good-by," said Richard. And then he added,
he hardly knew why, "Are you going to bid good-by
to Miss Whittaker?"

"Yes. Isn't she at home?"

Whether Richard really paused or not before he
answered, he never knew. There suddenly arose
such a tumult in his bosom that it seemed to him
several moments before he became conscious of his
reply. But it is probable that to Severn it came
only too soon.

"No," said Richard; "she's not at home. We
have just been calling." As he spoke, he shot a
glance at his companion, armed with defiance of his
impending denial. But the Major just met his
glance and then dropped his eyes. This slight motion was a horrible revelation. He had served the
Major, too.

"Ah? I'm sorry," said Severn, slacking his rein,

—"I'm sorry." And from his saddle he looked down toward the house more longingly and regretfully than he knew.

Richard felt himself turning from pale to consuming crimson. There was a simple sincerity in Severn's words which was almost irresistible. For a moment he felt like shouting out a loud denial of his falsehood: "She is there! she's alone and in tears, awaiting you. Go to her—and be damned!" But before he could gather his words into his throat, they were arrested by Major Luttrel's cool, clear voice, which, in its calmness, seemed to cast scorn upon his weakness.

"Captain," said the Major, "I shall be very happy to take charge of your farewell."

"Thank you, Major. Pray do. Say how extremely sorry I was. Good by again." And Captain Severn hastily turned his horse about, gave him his spurs, and galloped away, leaving his friends standing alone in the middle of the road. As the sound of his retreat expired, Richard, in spite of himself, drew a long breath. He sat motionless in the saddle, hanging his head.

"Mr. Clare," said the Major, at last, "that was very cleverly done."

Richard looked up. "I never told a lie before," said he.

"Upon my soul, then, you did it uncommonly well.

You did it so well I almost believed you. No wonder that Severn did."

Richard was silent. Then suddenly he broke out, "In God's name, sir, why don't you call me a blackguard? I've done a beastly act!"

"O, come," said the Major, "you needn't mind that, with me. We'll consider that said. I feel bound to let you know that I'm very, very much obliged to you. If you hadn't spoken, how do you know but that I might?"

"If you had, I would have given you the lie, square in your teeth."

"Would you, indeed? It's very fortunate, then, I held my tongue. If you will have it so, I won't deny that your little improvisation sounded very ugly. I'm devilish glad I didn't make it."

Richard felt his wit sharpened by a most unholy scorn,—a scorn far greater for his companion than for himself. "I am glad to hear that it did sound ugly," he said. "To me, it seemed beautiful, holy, and just. For the space of a moment, it seemed absolutely right that I should say what I did. But you saw the lie in its horrid nakedness, and yet you let it pass. You have no excuse."

"I beg your pardon. You are immensely ingenious, but you are immensely wrong. Are you going to make out that I am the guilty party? Upon my word, you're a cool hand. I *have* an excuse. I have the excuse of being interested in Miss Whittaker's remaining unengaged."

"So I suppose. But you don't love her. Otherwise——"

Major Luttrel laid his hand on Richard's bridle. "Mr. Clare," said he, "I have no wish to talk metaphysics over this matter. You had better say no more. I know that your feelings are not of an enviable kind, and I am therefore prepared to be goodnatured with you. But you must be civil yourself. You have done a shabby deed; you are ashamed of it, and you wish to shift the responsibility upon me, which is more shabby still. My advice is, that you behave like a man of spirit, and swallow your apprehensions. I trust that you are not going to make a fool of yourself by any apology or retraction in any quarter. As for its having seemed holy and just to do what you did, that is mere bosh. A lie is a lie, and as such is often excusable. As anything else,—as a thing beautiful, holy, or just,—it's quite inexcusable. Yours was a lie to you, and a lie to me. It serves me, and I accept it. I suppose you understand me. I adopt it. You don't suppose it was because I was frightened by those big black eyes of yours that I held my tongue. As for my loving or not loving Miss Whittaker, I have no report to make to you about it. I will simply say that I intend, if possible to marry her."

"She'll not have you. She'll never marry a cold-blooded rascal."

"I think she'll prefer him to a hot-blooded one. Do you want to pick a quarrel with me? Do you want to make me lose my temper? I shall refuse you that satisfaction. You have been a coward, and you want to frighten some one before you go to bed to make up for it. Strike me, and I'll strike you in self-defence, but I'm not going to mind your talk. Have you anything to say? No? Well, then, good evening." And Major Luttrel started away.

It was with rage that Richard was dumb. Had he been but a cat's-paw after all? Heaven forbid! He sat irresolute for an instant, and then turned suddenly and cantered back to Gertrude's gate. Here he stopped again; but after a short pause he went in over the gravel with a fast-beating heart. O, if Luttrel were but there to see him! For a moment he fancied he heard the sound of the Major's returning steps. If he would only come and find him at confession! It would be so easy to confess before him! He went along beside the house to the front, and stopped beneath the open drawing-room window.

"Gertrude!" he cried softly, from his saddle.

Gertrude immediately appeared. "You, Richard!" she exclaimed.

Her voice was neither harsh nor sweet; but her

words and her intonation recalled vividly to Richard's mind the scene in the conservatory. He fancied them keenly expressive of disappointment. He was invaded by a mischievous conviction that she had been expecting Captain Severn, or that at the least she had mistaken his voice for the Captain's. The truth is that she had half fancied it might be,— Richard's call having been little more than a loud whisper. The young man sat looking up at her, silent.

"What do you want?" she asked. "Can I do anything for you?"

Richard was not destined to do his duty that evening. A certain infinitesimal dryness of tone on Gertrude's part was the inevitable result of her finding that that whispered summons came only from Richard. She was preoccupied. Captain Severn had told her a fortnight before, that, in case of news of a defeat, he should not await the expiration of his leave of absence to return. Such news had now come, and her inference was that her friend would immediately take his departure. She could not but suppose that he would come and bid her farewell, and what might not be the incidents, the results, of such a visit? To tell the whole truth, it was under the pressure of these reflections that, twenty minutes before, Gertrude had dismissed our two gentlemen. That this long story should be told in the dozen words with which she greeted Richard, will seem unnatural to the disinterested reader. But in those words, poor Richard, with a lover's clairvoyance, read it at a single glance. The same resentful impulse, the same sickening of the heart, that he had felt in the conservatory, took possession of him once more. To be witness of Severn's passion for Gertrude,—that he could endure. To be witness of Gertrude's passion for Severn,—against that obligation his reason rebelled.

"What is it you wish, Richard?" Gertrude repeated. "Have you forgotten anything?"

"Nothing! nothing!" cried the young man. "It's no matter!"

He gave a great pull at his ·bridle, and almost brought his horse back on his haunches, and then, wheeling him about on himself, he thrust in his spurs and galloped out of the gate.

On the highway he came upon Major Luttrel, who stood looking down the lane.

"I'm going to the Devil, sir!" cried Richard. "Give me your hand on it."

Luttrel held out his hand. "My poor young man," said he, "you're out of your head. I'm sorry for you. You haven't been making a fool of yourself?"

"Yes, a damnable fool of myself!"

Luttrel breathed freely. "You'd better go home

and go to bed," he said. "You'll make yourself ill by going on at this rate."

"I—I'm afraid to go home," said Richard, in a broken voice. "For God's sake, come with me!"— and the wretched fellow burst into tears. "I'm too bad for any company but yours," he cried, in his sobs.

The Major winced, but he took pity. "Come, come," said he, "we'll pull through. I'll go home with you."

They rode off together. That night Richard went to bed miserably drunk; although Major Luttrel had left him at ten o'clock, adjuring him to drink no more. He awoke the next morning in a violent fever; and before evening the doctor, whom one of his hired men had brought to his bedside, had come and looked grave and pronounced him very ill.

PART III

In country districts, where life is quiet, incidents do duty as events; and accordingly Captain Severn's sudden departure for his regiment became very rapidly known among Gertrude's neighbors. She herself heard it from her coachman, who had heard it in the village, where the Captain had been seen to take the early train. She received the news calmly enough to outward appearance, but a great tumult rose and died in her breast. He had gone without a word of farewell! Perhaps he had not had time to call upon her. But bare civility would have dictated his dropping her a line of writing,—he who must have read in her eyes the feeling which her lips refused to utter, and who had been the object of her tenderest courtesy. It was not often that Gertrude threw back into her friends' teeth their acceptance of the hospitality which it had been placed in her power to offer them; but if she now mutely reproached Captain Severn with ingratitude, it was

138

because he had done more than slight her material gifts: he had slighted that constant moral force with which these gifts were accompanied, and of which they were but the rude and vulgar token. It is but natural to expect that our dearest friends will accredit us with our deepest feelings; and Gertrude had constituted Edmund Severn her dearest friend. She had not, indeed, asked his assent to this arrangement, but she had borne it out by a subtile devotion which she felt that she had a right to exact of him that he should repay,—repay by letting her know that, whether it was lost on his heart or not, it was at least not lost to his senses,—that, if he could not return it, he could at least remember it. She had given him the flower of her womanly tenderness, and when his moment came, he had turned from her without a look. Gertrude shed no tears. It seemed to her that she had given her friend tears enough, and that to expend her soul in weeping would be to wrong herself. She would think no more of Edmund Severn. He should be as little to her for the future as she was to him.

It was very easy to make this resolution: to keep it, Gertrude found another matter. She could not think of the war, she could not talk with her neighbors of current events, she could not take up a newspaper, without reverting to her absent friend. She found herself constantly harassed with the appre-

hension that he had not allowed himself time really
to recover, and that a fortnight's exposure would
send him back to the hospital. At last it occurred
to her that civility required that she should make a
call upon Mrs. Martin, the Captain's sister; and a
vague impression that this lady might be the deposi-
tary of some farewell message—perhaps of a letter—which she was awaiting her convenience to
present, led her at once to undertake this social
duty.

The carriage which had been ordered for her pro-
jected visit was at the door, when, within a week
after Severn's departure, Major Luttrel was announced. Gertrude received him in her bonnet.
His first care was to present Captain Severn's
adieus, together with his regrets that he had not had
time to discharge them in person. As Luttrel made
his speech, he watched his companion narrowly, and
was considerably reassured by the unflinching composure with which she listened to it. The turn he
had given to Severn's message had been the fruit
of much mischievous cogitation. It had seemed to
him that, for his purposes, the assumption of a hasty,
and as it were mechanical, allusion to Miss Whittaker, was more serviceable than the assumption of
no allusion at all, which would have left a boundless
void for the exercise of Gertrude's fancy. And he
had reasoned well; for although he was tempted to

infer from her calmness that his shot had fallen
short of the mark, yet, in spite of her silent and almost smiling assent to his words, it had made but
one bound to her heart. Before many minutes, she
felt that those words had done her a world of good.
"He had not had time!" Indeed, as she took to herself their full expression of perfect indifference, she
felt that her hard, forced smile was broadening into
the sign of a lively gratitude to the Major.

Major Luttrel had still another task to perform.
He had spent half an hour on the preceding day at
Richard's bedside, having ridden over to the farm,
in ignorance of his illness, to see how matters stood
with him. The reader will already have surmised
that the Major was not pre-eminently a man of conscience: he will, therefore, be the less surprised and
shocked to hear that the sight of the poor young
man, prostrate, fevered, and delirious, and to all appearance rapidly growing worse, filled him with an
emotion the reverse of creditable. In plain terms,
he was very glad to find Richard a prisoner in bed.
He had been racking his brains for a scheme to keep
his young friend out of the way, and now, to his
exceeding satisfaction, Nature had relieved him of
this troublesome care. If Richard was condemned
to typhoid fever, which his symptoms seemed to
indicate, he would not, granting his recovery, be
able to leave his room within a month. In a month,

much might be done; nay, with energy, all might be done. The reader has been all but directly informed that the Major's present purpose was to secure Miss Whittaker's hand. He was poor, and he was ambitious, and he was, moreover, so well advanced in life—being thirty-six years of age—that he had no heart to think of building up his fortune by slow degrees. A man of good breeding, too, he had become sensible, as he approached middle age of the many advantages of a luxurious home. He had accordingly decided that a wealthy marriage would most easily unlock the gate to prosperity. A girl of a somewhat lighter calibre than Gertrude would have been the woman—we cannot say of his heart; but, as he very generously argued, beggars can't be choosers. Gertrude was a woman with a mind of her own; but, on the whole, he was not afraid of her. He was abundantly prepared to do his duty. He had, of course, as became a man of sense, duly weighed his obstacles against his advantages; but an impartial scrutiny had found the latter heavier in the balance. The only serious difficulty in his path was the possibility that, on hearing of Richard's illness, Gertrude, with her confounded benevolence, would take a fancy to nurse him in person, and that, in the course of her ministrations, his delirious ramblings would force upon her mind the damning story of the deception practised upon Cap-

tain Severn. There was nothing for it but bravely
to face this risk. As for that other fact, which many
men of a feebler spirit would have deemed an invincible obstacle, Luttrel's masterly understanding
had immediately converted it into the prime agent
of success,—the fact, namely, that Gertrude's heart
was preoccupied. Such knowledge as he possessed
of the relations between Miss Whittaker and his
brother officer he had gained by his unaided observa-
tions and his silent deductions. These had been
logical; for, on the whole, his knowledge was accu-
rate. It was at least what he might have termed a
good working knowledge. He had calculated on a
passionate reactionary impulse on Gertrude's part,
consequent on Severn's simulated offence. He knew
that, in a generous woman, such an impulse, if left
to itself, would not go very far. But on this point
it was that his policy bore. He would not leave it
to itself: he would take it gently into his hands,
attenuate it, prolong it, economize it, and mould it
into the clew to his own good-fortune. He thus
counted much upon his skill and his tact; but he
likewise placed a becoming degree of reliance upon
his solid personal qualities,—qualities too sober and
too solid, perhaps, to be called *charms,* but thoroughly adapted to inspire confidence. The Major
was not handsome in feature; he left that to younger
men and to lighter women; but his ugliness was

of a masculine, aristocratic, intelligent stamp. His figure, moreover, was good enough to compensate for the absence of a straight nose and a fine mouth; and his general bearing offered a most pleasing combination of the gravity of the man of affairs and the versatility of the man of society.

In her sudden anxiety on Richard's behalf, Gertrude soon forgot her own immaterial woes. The carriage which was to have conveyed her to Mrs. Martin's was used for a more disinterested purpose. The Major, prompted by a strong faith in the salutary force of his own presence, having obtained her permission to accompany her, they set out for the farm, and soon found themselves in Richard's chamber. The young man was wrapped in a heavy sleep, from which it was judged imprudent to arouse him. Gertrude, sighing as she compared his thinly furnished room with her own elaborate apartments, drew up a mental list of essential luxuries which she would immediately send him. Not but that he had received, however, a sufficiency of homely care. The doctor was assiduous, and the old woman who nursed him was full of rough good-sense.

"He asks very often after you, Miss," she said, addressing Gertrude, but with a sly glance at the Major. "But I think you'd better not come too often. I'm afraid you'd excite him more than you'd quiet him."

"I'm afraid you would, Miss Whittaker," said the Major, who could have hugged the goodwife.

"Why should I excite him?" asked Gertrude, "I'm used to sick-rooms. I nursed my father for a year and a half."

"O, it's very well for an old woman like me, but it's no place for a fine young lady like you," said the nurse, looking at Gertrude's muslins and laces.

"I'm not so fine as to desert a friend in distress," said Gertrude. "I shall come again, and if it makes the poor fellow worse to see me, I shall stay away. I am ready to do anything that will help him to get well."

It had already occurred to her that, in his unnatural state, Richard might find her presence a source of irritation, and she was prepared to remain in the background. As she returned to her carriage, she caught herself reflecting with so much pleasure upon Major Luttrel's kindness in expending a couple of hours of his valuable time on so unprofitable an object as poor Richard, that, by way of intimating her satisfaction, she invited him to come home and dine with her.

After a short interval she paid Richard a second visit, in company with Miss Pendexter. He was a great deal worse; he lay emaciated, exhausted, and stupid. The issue was doubtful. Gertrude immediately pushed forward to M——, a larger town than her own, sought out a professional nurse, and arranged with him to relieve the old woman from the farm, who was worn out with her vigilance. For a fortnight, moreover, she received constant tidings from the young man's physician. During this fortnight, Major Luttrel was assiduous, and proportionately successful.

It may be said, to his credit, that he had by no means conducted his suit upon that narrow programme which he had drawn up at the outset. He very soon discovered that Gertrude's resentment— if resentment there was—was a substance utterly impalpable even to his most delicate tact, and he had accordingly set to work to woo her like an honest man, from day to day, from hour to hour, trusting so devoutly for success to momentary inspiration, that he felt his suit dignified by a certain flattering *faux air* of genuine passion. He occasionally reminded himself, however, that he might really be owing more to the subtle force of accidental contrast than Gertrude's life-long reserve—for it was certain she would not depart from it—would ever allow him to measure.

It was as an honest man, then, a man of impulse and of action, that Gertrude had begun to like him. She was not slow to perceive whither his operations tended; and she was almost tempted at times to tell him frankly that she would spare him the intermediate steps, and meet him at the goal without further delay. It was not that she was prepared to love him, but she would make him an obedient wife. An immense weariness had somehow come upon her, and a sudden sense of loneliness. A vague suspicion that her money had done her an incurable wrong inspired her with a profound distaste for the care of it. She felt cruelly hedged out from human sympathy by her bristling possessions. "If I had had five hundred dollars a year," she said in a frequent parenthesis, "I might have pleased him." Hating her wealth, accordingly, and chilled by her isolation, the temptation was strong upon her to give herself up to that wise, brave gentleman who seemed to have adopted such a happy medium betwixt loving her for her money and fearing her for it. Would she not always stand between men who would represent the two extremes? She would anticipate security by an alliance with Major Luttrel.

One evening, on presenting himself, Luttrel read these thoughts so clearly in her eyes, that he made up his mind to speak. But his mind was burdened with a couple of facts, of which it was necessary that he should discharge it before it could enjoy the freedom of action which the occasion required. In the first place, then, he had been to see Richard Clare, and had found him suddenly and decidedly better. It was unbecoming, however,—it was im-

possible,—that he should allow Gertrude to linger
over this pleasant announcement.

"I tell the good news first," he said, gravely. "I
have some very bad news, too, Miss Whittaker."

Gertrude sent him a rapid glance. "Some one has
been killed," she said.

"Captain Severn has been shot," said the Major,
—"shot by a guerilla."

Gertrude was silent. No answer seemed possible
to that uncompromising fact. She sat with her head
on her hand, and her elbow on the table beside her,
looking at the figures on the carpet. She uttered no
words of commonplace regret; but she felt as little
like giving way to serious grief. She had lost nothing, and, to the best of her knowledge, *he* had lost
nothing. She had an old loss to mourn,—a loss a
month old, which she had mourned as she might.
To give way to passion would have been but to impugn the solemnity of her past regrets. When she
looked up at her companion, she was pale, but she
was calm, yet with a calmness upon which a single
glance of her eye directed him not inconsiderately
to presume. She was aware that this glance betrayed her secret; but in view both of Severn's death
and of the Major's attitude, such betrayal mattered
less. Luttrel had prepared to act upon her hint, and
to avert himself gently from the topic, when Gertrude, who had dropped her eyes again, raised them

with a slight shudder. "I'm cold," she said. "Will you shut that window beside you, Major? Or stay, suppose you give me my shawl from the sofa."

Luttrel brought the shawl, placed it on her shoulders, and sat down beside her. "These are cruel times," he said, with studied simplicity. "I'm sure I hardly know what's to come of it all."

"Yes, they are cruel times," said Gertrude. "They make one feel cruel. They make one doubt of all he has learnt from his pastors and masters."

"Yes, but they teach us something new also."

"I'm sure I don't know," said Gertrude, whose heart was so full of bitterness that she felt almost malignant. "They teach us how mean we are. War is an infamy, Major, though it *is* your trade. It's very well for you, who look at it professionally, and for those who go and fight; but it's a miserable business for those who stay at home, and do the thinking and the sentimentalizing. It's a miserable business for women; it makes us more spiteful than ever."

"Well, a little spite isn't a bad thing, in practice," said the Major. "War is certainly an abomination, both at home and in the field. But as wars go, Miss Whittaker, our own is a very satisfactory one. It involves something. It won't leave us as it found us. We're in the midst of a revolution, and what's a revolution but a turning upside down? It makes sad work with our habits and theories and our tradi-

tions and convictions. But, on the other hand,"
Luttrel pursued, warming to his task, "it leaves
something untouched, which is better than these,—
I mean our feelings, Miss Whittaker." And the
Major paused until he had caught Gertrude's eyes,
when, having engaged them with his own, he proceeded. "I think they are the stronger for the down-
fall of so much else, and, upon my soul, I think it's
in them we ought to take refuge. Don't you think
so?"

"Yes, if I understand you."

"I mean our serious feelings, you know,—not our
tastes nor our passions. I don't advocate fiddling
while Rome is burning. In fact it's only poor, un-
satisfied devils that are tempted to fiddle. There is
one feeling which is respectable and honorable, and
even sacred, at all times and in all places, whatever
they may be. It doesn't depend upon circumstances,
but they upon it; and with its help, I think, we are a
match for any circumstances. I don't mean religion,
Miss Whittaker," added the Major, with a sober
smile.

"If you don't mean religion," said Gertrude, "I
suppose you mean love. That's a very different
thing."

"Yes, a very different thing; so I've always
thought, and so I'm glad to hear you say. Some
people, you know, mix them up in the most extraor-

dinary fashion. I don't fancy myself an especially
religious man; in fact, I believe I'm rather otherwise. It's my nature. Half mankind are born so,
or I suppose the affairs of this world wouldn't
move. But I believe I'm a good lover, Miss Whittaker."

"I hope for your own sake you are, Major Luttrel."

"Thank you. Do you think now you could entertain the idea for the sake of any one else?"

Gertrude neither dropped her eyes, nor shrugged
her shoulders, nor blushed. If anything, indeed,
she turned somewhat paler than before, as she sustained her companion's gaze, and prepared to answer him as directly as she might.

"If I loved you, Major Luttrel," she said, "I
should value the idea for my own sake."

The Major, too, blanched a little. "I put my
question conditionally," he answered, "and I have
got, as I deserved, a conditional reply. I will speak
plainly, then, Miss Whittaker. *Do* you value the
fact for your own sake? It would be plainer still
to say, Do you love me? but I confess I'm not brave
enough for that. I will say, Can you? or I will
even content myself with putting it in the conditional again, and asking you if you could; although,
after all, I hardly know what the *if* understood can
reasonably refer to. I'm not such a fool as to ask

of any woman—least of all of you—to love me contingently. You can only answer for the present, and say yes or no. I shouldn't trouble you to say either, if I didn't conceive that I had given you time to make up your mind. It doesn't take forever to know James Luttrel. I'm not one of the great unfathomable ones. We've seen each other more or less intimately for a good many weeks; and as I'm conscious, Miss Whittaker, of having shown you my best, I take it for granted that if you don't fancy me now, you won't a month hence, when you shall have seen my faults. Yes, Miss Whittaker, I can solemnly say," continued the Major, with genuine feeling, "I have shown you my best, as every man is in honor bound to do who approaches a woman with those predispositions with which I have approached you. I have striven hard to please you," —and he paused. "I can only say, I hope I have succeeded."

"I should be very insensible," said Gertrude, "if all your kindness and your courtesy had been lost upon me."

"In Heaven's name, don't talk about courtesy," cried the Major.

"I am deeply conscious of your devotion, and I am very much obliged to you for urging your claims so respectfully and considerately. I speak seriously, Major Luttrel," pursued Gertrude. "There is a happy medium of expression, and you have taken it. Now it seems to me that there is a happy medium of affection, with which you might be content. Strictly, I don't love you. I question my heart, and it gives me that answer. The feeling that I have is not a feeling to work prodigies."

"May it at least work the prodigy of allowing you to be my wife?"

"I don't think I shall over-estimate its strength, if I say that it may. If you can respect a woman who gives you her hand in cold blood, you are welcome to mine."

Luttrel moved his chair and took her hand. "Beggars can't be choosers," said he, raising it to his mustache.

"O Major Luttrel, don't say that," she answered. "I give you a great deal; but I keep a little,—a little," said Gertrude, hesitating, "which I suppose I shall give to God."

"Well, I shall not be jealous," said Luttrel.

"The rest I give to you, and in return I ask a great deal."

"I shall give you all. You know I told you I'm not religious."

"No, I don't want more than I give," said Gertrude.

"But, pray," asked Luttrel, with a delicate smile, "what am I to do with the difference?"

"You had better keep it for yourself. What I want is your protection, sir, and your advice, and your care. I want you to take me away from this place, even if you have to take me down to the army. I want to see the world under the shelter of your name. I shall give you a great deal of trouble. I'm a mere mass of possessions: what I am, is nothing to what I have. But ever since I began to grow up, what I am has been the slave of what I have. I am weary of my chains, and you must help me to carry them,"—and Gertrude rose to her feet as if to inform the Major that his audience was at an end.

He still held her right hand; she gave him the other. He stood looking down at her, an image of manly humility, while from his silent breast went out a brief thanksgiving to favoring fortune.

At the pressure of his hands, Gertrude felt her bosom heave. She burst into tears. "O, you must be very kind to me!" she cried, as he put his arm about her, and she dropped her head upon his shoulder.

When once Richard's health had taken a turn for the better, it began very rapidly to improve. "Until he is quite well," Gertrude said, one day, to her accepted suitor, "I had rather he heard nothing of our engagement. He was once in love with me himself," she added, very frankly. "Did you ever suspect it? But I hope he will have got better of that sad malady, too. Nevertheless, I shall expect nothing of his good judgment until he is quite strong; and as he may hear of my new intentions from other people, I propose that, for the present, we confide them to no one."

"But if he asks me point-blank," said the Major, "what shall I answer?"

"It's not likely he'll ask you. How should he suspect anything?"

"O," said Luttrel, "Clare is one that suspects everything."

"Tell him we're not engaged, then. A woman in my position may say what she pleases."

It was agreed, however, that certain preparations for the marriage should meanwhile go forward in secret; and that the marriage itself should take place in August, as Luttrel expected to be ordered back into service in the autumn. At about this moment Gertrude was surprised to receive a short note from Richard, so feebly scrawled in pencil as to be barely legible. "Dear Gertrude, it ran, "don't come to see me just yet. I'm not fit. You would hurt me, and *vice versa*. God bless you! R. CLARE." Miss Whittaker explained his request, by the supposition that a report had come to him of Major Luttrel's late assiduities (which it was impossible should go unobserved); that, leaping at the worst, he had taken her engagement for granted; and that, under this impression, he could not trust himself to see her. She despatched him an answer, telling him that she would await his pleasure, and that, if the doctor would consent to his having letters, she would meanwhile occasionally write to him. "She will give me good advice," thought Richard impatiently; and on this point, accordingly, she received no account of his wishes. Expecting to leave her house and close it on her marriage, she spent many hours in wandering sadly over the meadow-paths and through the woodlands which she had known from her childhood. She had thrown aside the last ensigns of filial regret, and now walked sad and splendid in the uncompromising colors of an affianced bride. It would have seemed to a stranger that, for a woman who had freely chosen a companion for life, she was amazingly spiritless and sombre. As she looked at her pale cheeks and heavy eyes in the mirror, she felt ashamed that she had no fairer countenance to offer to her destined lord. She had lost her single beauty, her smile; and she would make but a ghastly figure at the altar. "I ought to wear a calico dress and an apron," she said to herself, "and not this glaring finery." But she continued to wear her finery, and to lay out her money, and to perform all her old duties to the letter. After the lapse of what she deemed a sufficient interval, she went to see Mrs. Martin, and to listen dumbly to her narration of her brother's death, and to her simple eulogies.

Major Luttrel performed his part quite as bravely, and much more successfully. He observed neither too many things nor too few; he neither presumed upon his success, nor mistrusted it. Having on his side received no prohibition from Richard, he resumed his visits at the farm, trusting that, with the return of reason, his young friend might feel disposed to renew that anomalous alliance in which, on the hapless evening of Captain Severn's farewell, he had taken refuge against his despair. In the long, languid hours of his early convalescence, Richard had found time to survey his position, to summon back piece by piece the immediate past, and to frame a general scheme for the future. But more vividly than anything else, there had finally disengaged itself from his meditations a profound aversion to James Luttrel.

It was in this humor that the Major found him; and as he looked at the young man's gaunt shoulders, supported by pillows, at his face, so livid and aquiline, at his great dark eyes, luminous with triumphant life, it seemed to him that an invincible spirit had been sent from a better world to breathe confusion upon his hopes. If Richard hated the

Major, the reader may guess whether the Major loved Richard. Luttrel was amazed at his first remark.

"I suppose you're engaged by this time," Richard said, calmly enough.

"Not quite," answered the Major. "There's a chance for you yet."

To this Richard made no rejoinder. Then, suddenly, "Have you had any news of Captain Severn?" he asked.

For a moment the Major was perplexed at his question. He had assumed that the news of Severn's death had come to Richard's ears, and he had been half curious, half apprehensive as to its effect. But an instant's reflection now assured him that the young man's estrangement from his neighbors had kept him hitherto and might still keep him in ignorance of the truth. Hastily, therefore, and inconsiderately, the Major determined to confirm this ignorance. "No," said he; "I've had no news. Severn and I are not on such terms as to correspond."

The next time Luttrel came to the farm, he found the master sitting up in a great, cushioned, chintz-covered arm-chair which Gertrude had sent him the day before out of her own dressing-room.

"Are you engaged yet?" asked Richard.

There was a strain as if of defiance in his tone.

The Major was irritated. "Yes," said he, "we are engaged now."

The young man's face betrayed no emotion.

"Are you reconciled to it?" asked Luttrel.

"Yes, practically I am."

"What do you mean by practically? Explain yourself."

"A man in my state can't explain himself. I mean that, however I feel about it, I shall accept Gertrude's marriage."

"You're a wise man, my boy," said the Major, kindly.

"I'm growing wise. I feel like Solomon on his throne in this chair. But I confess, sir, I don't see how she could have you."

"Well, there's no accounting for tastes," said the Major, good-humoredly.

"Ah, if it's been a matter of taste with her," said Richard, "I have nothing to say."

They came to no more express understanding than this with regard to the future. Richard continued to grow stronger daily, and to defer the renewal of his intercourse with Gertrude. A month before, he would have resented as a bitter insult the intimation that he would ever be so resigned to lose her as he now found himself. He would not see her for two reasons: first, because he felt that it would be—or that at least in reason it ought to be—a painful

experience to look upon his old mistress with a coldly
critical eye; and secondly, because, justify to himself
as he would his new-born indifference, he could not
entirely cast away the suspicion that it was a last
remnant of disease, and that, when he stood on his
legs again in the presence of those exuberant land-
scapes with which he had long since established a
sort of sensuous communion, he would feel, as with
a great tumultuous rush, the return of his impetuous
manhood and of his old capacity. When he had
smoked a pipe in the outer sunshine, when he had
settled himself once more to the long elastic bound
of his mare, then he would see Gertrude. The
reason of the change which had come upon him
was that she had disappointed him,—she, whose
magnanimity it had once seemed that his fancy was
impotent to measure. She had accepted Major Luttrel, a man whom he despised; she had so mutilated her magnificent heart as to match it with his.
The validity of his dislike to the Major, Richard did
not trouble himself to examine. He accepted it as
an unerring instinct; and, indeed, he might have
asked himself, had he not sufficient proof? Moreover he labored under the sense of a gratuitous
wrong. He had suffered an immense torment of
remorse to drive him into brutishness, and thence to
the very gate of death, for an offence which he had
deemed mortal, and which was after all but a phan-

tasm of his impassioned conscience. What a fool he had been! a fool for his nervous fears, and a fool for his penitence. Marriage with Major Luttrel,—such was the end of Gertrude's fancied anguish. Such, too, we hardly need add, was the end of that idea of reparation which had been so formidable to Luttrel. Richard had been generous; he would now be just.

Far from impeding his recovery, these reflections hastened it. One morning in the beginning of August, Gertrude received notice of Richard's presence. It was a still, sultry day, and Miss Whittaker, her habitual pallor deepened by the oppressive heat, was sitting alone in a white morning-dress, languidly fanning aside at once the droning flies and her equally importunate thoughts. She found Richard standing in the middle of the drawing-room, booted and spurred.

"Well, Richard," she exclaimed, with some feeling, "you're at last willing to see me!"

As his eyes fell upon her, he started and stood almost paralyzed, heeding neither her words nor her extended hand. It was not Gertrude he saw, but her ghost.

"In Heaven's name what has happened to you?" he cried. "Have *you* been ill?"

Gertrude tried to smile in feigned surprise at his surprise; but her muscles relaxed. Richard's words and looks reflected more vividly than any mirror the dejection of her person; and this, the misery of her soul. She felt herself growing faint. She staggered back to a sofa and sank down.

Then Richard felt as if the room were revolving about him, and as if his throat were choked with imprecations,—as if his old erratic passion had again taken possession of him, like a mingled legion of devils and angels. It was through pity that his love returned. He went forward and dropped on his knees at Gertrude's feet. "Speak to me!" he cried, seizing her hands. "Are you unhappy? Is your heart broken? O Gertrude! what have you come to?"

Gertrude drew her hands from his grasp and rose to her feet. "Get up, Richard," she said. "Don't talk so wildly. I'm not well. I'm very glad to see you. *You* look well."

"I've got my strength again,—and meanwhile you've been failing. You're unhappy, you're wretched! Don't say you're not, Gertrude: it's as plain as day. You're breaking your heart."

"The same old Richard!" said Gertrude, trying to smile again.

"Would that you were the same old Gertrude! Don't try to smile; you can't!"

"I *shall!*" said Gertrude, desperately. "I'm going to be married, you know."

"Yes, I know. I don't congratulate you."

"I have not counted upon that honor, Richard. I shall have to do without it."

"You'll have to do without a great many things!" cried Richard, horrified by what seemed to him her blind self-immolation.

"I have all I ask," said Gertrude.

"You haven't all *I* ask then! You haven't all your friends ask."

"My friends are very kind, but I marry to suit myself."

"You've not suited yourself!" retorted the young man. "You've suited—God knows what!—your pride, your despair, your resentment." As he looked at her, the secret history of her weakness seemed to become plain to him, and he felt a mighty rage against the man who had taken a base advantage of it. "Gertrude!" he cried, "I entreat you to go back. It's not for my sake,—I'll give you up,— I'll go a thousand miles away, and never look at you again. It's for your own. In the name of your happiness, break with that man! Don't fling yourself away. Buy him off, if you consider yourself bound. Give him your money. That's all he wants."

As Gertrude listened, the blood came back to her face, and two flames into her eyes. She looked at Richard from head to foot. "You are not weak,"

she said, "you are in your senses, you are well and
strong; you shall tell me what you mean. You
insult the best friend I have. Explain yourself! you
insinuate foul things,—speak them out!" Her eyes
glanced toward the door, and Richard's followed
them. Major Luttrel stood on the threshold.

"Come in, sir!" cried Richard. "Gertrude swears
she'll believe no harm of you. Come and tell her
that she's wrong! How can you keep on harassing
a woman whom you've brought to this state? Think
of what she was three months ago, and look at
her now!"

Luttrel received this broadside without flinching.
He had overheard Richard's voice from the entry,
and he had steeled his heart for the encounter. He
assumed the air of having been so amazed by the
young man's first words as only to have heard his
last; and he glanced at Gertrude mechanically as if
to comply with them. "What's the matter?" he
asked, going over to her, and taking her hand; "are
you ill?" Gertrude let him have her hand, but she
forbore to meet his eyes.

"Ill! of course she's ill!" cried Richard, passionately. "She's dying,—she's consuming herself! I
know I seem to be playing an odious part here,
Gertrude, but, upon my soul, I can't help it. I look
like a betrayer, an informer, a sneak, but I don't
feel like one! Still, I'll leave you, if you say so."

"Shall he go, Gertrude?" asked Luttrel, without looking at Richard.

"No. Let him stay and explain himself. He has accused you,—let him prove his case."

"I know what he is going to say," said Luttrel. "It will place me in a bad light. Do you still wish to hear it?"

Gertrude drew her hand hastily out of Luttrel's. "Speak, Richard!" she cried, with a passionate gesture.

"I will speak," said Richard. "I've done you a dreadful wrong, Gertrude. How great a wrong, I never knew until I saw you to-day so miserably altered. When I heard that you were to be married, I fancied that it was no wrong, and that my remorse had been wasted. But I understand it now; and *he* understands it, too. You once told me that you had ceased to love Captain Severn. It wasn't true. You never ceased to love him. You love him at this moment. If he were to get another wound in the next battle, how would you feel? How would you bear it?" And Richard paused for an instant with the force of his interrogation.

"For God's sake," cried Gertrude, "respect the dead!"

"The dead! Is he dead?"

Gertrude covered her face with her hands.

"You beast!" cried Luttrel.

Richard turned upon him savagely. "Shut your infernal mouth!" he roared. "You told me he was alive and well!"

Gertrude made a movement of speechless distress.

"You would have it, my dear," said Luttrel, with a little bow.

Richard had turned pale, and began to tremble. "Excuse me, Gertrude," he said hoarsely, "I've been deceived. Poor, unhappy woman! Gertrude," he continued, going nearer to her, and speaking in a whisper, "*I* killed him."

Gertrude fell back from him, as he approached her, with a look of unutterable horror. "I and *he*," said Richard, pointing at Luttrel.

Gertrude's eyes followed the direction of his gesture, and transferred their scorching disgust to her suitor. This was too much for Luttrel's courage. "You idiot!" she shouted at Richard, "speak out!"

"He loved you, though you believed he didn't," said Richard. "I saw it the first time I looked at him. To every one but you it was as plain as day. Luttrel saw it, too. But he was too modest, and he never fancied you cared for him. The night before he went back to the army, he came to bid you good-by. If he had seen you, it would have been better for every one. You remember that evening, of course. We met him, Luttrel and I. He was all

on fire,—he meant to speak. I knew it ; you knew it,
Luttrel : it was in his fingers' ends. I intercepted
him. I turned him off,—I lied to him and told him
you were away. I was a coward, and I did neither
more nor less than that. I knew you were waiting
for him. It was stronger than my will,—I believe
I should do it again. Fate was against him, and
he went off. I came back to tell you, but my damnable jealousy strangled me. I went home and drank
myself into a fever. I've done you a wrong that I
can never repair. I'd go hang myself if I thought it
would help you." Richard spoke slowly, softly, and
explicitly, as if irresistible Justice in person had
her hand upon his neck, and were forcing him down
upon his knees. In the presence of Gertrude's dis-
may nothing seemed possible but perfect self-convic-
tion. In Luttrel's attitude, as he stood with his head
erect, his arms folded, and his cold, gray eyes fixed
upon the distance, it struck him that there was something atrociously insolent; not insolent to him,—
for that he cared little enough,—but insolent to Gertrude and to the dreadful solemnity of the hour.
Richard sent the Major a look of the most aggressive contempt. "As for Major Luttrel," he said,
"*he* was but a passive spectator. No, Gertrude, by
Heaven!" he burst out, "he was worse than I! I
loved you, and he didn't!"

"Our friend is correct in his facts, Gertrude,"

said Luttrel, quietly. "He is incorrect in his opinions. I *was* a passive spectator of his deception. He appeared to enjoy a certain authority with regard to your wishes,—the source of which I respected both of you sufficiently never to question, —and I accepted the act which he has described as an exercise of it. You will remember that you had sent us away on the ground that you were in no humor for company. To deny you, therefore, to another visitor, seemed to me rather officious, but still pardonable. You will consider that I was wholly ignorant of your relations to that visitor; that whatever you may have done for others, Gertrude, to me you never vouchsafed a word of information on the subject, and that Mr. Clare's words are a revelation to me. But I am bound to believe nothing that he says. I am bound to believe that I have injured you only when I hear it from your own lips."

Richard made a movement as if to break out upon the Major; but Gertrude, who had been standing motionless with her eyes upon the ground, quickly raised them, and gave him a look of imperious prohibition. She had listened, and she had chosen. She turned to Luttrel. "Major Luttrel," she said, "you *have* been an accessory in what has been for me a serious grief. It is my duty to tell you so. I mean, of course, a profoundly unwilling accessory. I pity you more than I can tell you. I think your position more pitiable than mine. It is true that I never made a confidant of you. I never made one of Richard. I had a secret, and he surprised it. You were less fortunate." It might have seemed to a thoroughly dispassionate observer that in these last four words there was an infinitesimal touch of tragic irony. Gertrude paused a moment while Luttrel eyed her intently, and Richard, from a somewhat tardy instinct of delicacy, walked over to the bow-window. "This is the most painful moment of my life," she resumed. "I hardly know where my duty lies. The only thing that is plain to me is, that I must ask you to release me from my engagement. I ask it most humbly, Major Luttrel," Gertrude continued, with warmth in her words, and a chilling coldness in her voice,—a coldness which it sickened her to feel there, but which she was unable to dispel. "I can't expect that you should give me up easily; I know that it's a great deal to ask, and"—she forced the chosen words out of her mouth—"I should thank you more than I can say if you would put some condition upon my release. You have done honorably by me, and I repay you with ingratitude. But I can't marry you." Her voice began to melt. "I have been false from the beginning. I have no heart to give you. I should make you a despicable wife."

The Major, too, had listened and chosen, and in this trying conjecture he set the seal to his character as an accomplished man. He saw that Gertrude's movement was final, and he determined to respect the inscrutable mystery of her heart. He read in the glance of her eye and the tone of her voice that the perfect dignity had fallen from his character,—that his integrity had lost its bloom; but he also read her firm resolve never to admit this fact to her own mind, nor to declare it to the world, and he honored her forbearance. His hopes, his ambitions, his visions, lay before him like a colossal heap of broken glass; but he would be as graceful as she was. She had divined him; but she had spared him. The Major was inspired.

"You have at least spoken to the point," he said. "You leave no room for doubt or for hope. With the little light I have, I can't say I understand your feelings, but I yield to them religiously. I believe so thoroughly that you suffer from the thought of what you ask of me, that I will not increase your suffering by assuring you of my own. I care for nothing but your happiness. You have lost it, and I give you mine to replace it. And although it's a simple thing to say," he added, "I must say simply that I thank you for your implicit faith in my integrity,"—and he held out his hand. As she gave him hers, Gertrude felt utterly in the wrong; and she looked into his eyes with an expression so humble, so appealing, so grateful, that, after all, his exit may be called triumphant.

When he had gone, Richard turned from the window with an enormous sense of relief. He had heard Gertrude's speech, and he knew that perfect justice had not been done; but still there was enough to be thankful for. Yet now that his duty was accomplished, he was conscious of a sudden lassitude. Mechanically he looked at Gertrude, and almost mechanically he came towards her. She, on her side, looking at him as he walked slowly down the long room, his face indistinct against the deadened light of the white-draped windows behind him, marked the expression of his figure with another pang. "He has rescued me," she said to herself; "but his passion has perished in the tumult. Richard," she said aloud, uttering the first words of vague kindness that came into her mind, "I forgive you."

Richard stopped. The idea had lost its charm. "You're very kind," he said, wearily. "You're far too kind. How do you know you forgive me? Wait and see."

Gertrude looked at him as she had never looked before; but he saw nothing of it. He saw a sad, plain girl in a white dress, nervously handling her fan. He was thinking of himself. If he had been thinking of her, he would have read in her lingering,

upward gaze, that he had won her; and if, so reading, he had opened his arms, Gertrude would have
come to them. We trust the reader is not shocked.
She neither hated him nor despised him, as she
ought doubtless in consistency to have done. She
felt that he was abundantly a man, and she loved
him. Richard, on his side, felt humbly the same
truth, and he began to respect himself. The past
had closed abruptly behind him, and tardy Gertrude
had been shut in. The future was dimly shaping
itself without her image. So he did not open his
arms.

"Good-by," he said, holding out his hand. "I
may not see you again for a long time."

Gertrude felt as if the world were deserting her.
"Are you going away?" she asked, tremulously.

"I mean to sell out and pay my debts, and go to
the war."

She gave him her hand, and he silently shook it.
There was no contending with the war, and she
gave him up.

With their separation our story properly ends,
and to say more would be to begin a new story. It
is, perhaps, our duty, however, expressly to add,
that Major Luttrel, in obedience to a logic of his
own, abstained from revenge; and that, if time has
not avenged him, it has at least rewarded him. General Luttrel, who lost an arm before the war was

over, recently married Miss Van Winkel of Philadelphia, and seventy thousand a year. Richard engaged in the defence of his country, on a captain's
commission, obtained with some difficulty. He saw
a great deal of fighting, but he has no scars to
show. The return of peace found him in his native
place, without a home, and without resources. One
of his first acts was to call dutifully and respectfully
upon Miss Whittaker, whose circle of acquaintance
had apparently become very much enlarged, and
now included a vast number of gentlemen. Gertrude's manner was kindness itself, but a more
studied kindness than before. She had lost much
of her youth and her simplicity. Richard wondered
whether she had pledged herself to spinsterhood,
but, of course, he didn't ask her. She inquired very
particularly into his material prospects and intentions, and offered most urgently to lend him money,
which he declined to borrow. When he left her,
he took a long walk through her place and beside
the river, and, wandering back to the days when
he had yearned for her love, assured himself that
no woman would ever again be to him what she had
been. During his stay in this neighborhood he
found himself impelled to a species of submission
to one of the old agricultural magnates whom he
had insulted in his unregenerate days, and through
whom he was glad to obtain some momentary em-

ployment. But his present position is very distasteful to him, and he is eager to try his fortunes in the West. As yet, however, he has lacked even the means to get as far as St. Louis. He drinks no more than is good for him. To speak of Gertrude's impressions of Richard would lead us quite too far. Shortly after his return she broke up her household, and came to the bold resolution (bold, that is, for a woman young, unmarried, and ignorant of manners in her own country) to spend some time in Europe. At our last accounts she was living in the ancient city of Florence. Her great wealth, of which she was wont to complain that it excluded her from human sympathy, now affords her a most efficient protection. She passes among her fellow-countrymen abroad for a very independent, but a very happy woman; although, as she is by this time twenty-seven years of age, a little romance is occasionally invoked to account for her continued celibacy.

III

A DAY OF DAYS

A DAY OF DAYS

Mr. Herbert Moore, a gentleman of some note in the scientific world, and a childless widower, finding himself at last unable to reconcile his sedentary habits with the management of a household, had invited his only sister to come and superintend his domestic affairs. Miss Adela Moore had assented the more willingly to his proposal, as by her mother's death she had recently been left without a formal protector. She was twenty-five years of age, and was a very active member of what she and her friends called society. She was almost equally at home in the very best company of three great cities, and she had encountered most of the adventures which await a young girl on the threshold of life. She had become rather hastily and imprudently engaged, but she had eventually succeeded in disengaging herself. She had spent a summer in Europe, and she had made a voyage to Cuba with a dear friend in the last stage of consumption, who had died at the hotel in Havana. Although by no means beautiful in person, she was yet thoroughly pleasing, rejoicing in what young ladies are fond of calling an *air*. That is, she was tall and slender, with a long neck, a low forehead and a handsome nose. Even after six years of "society," too, she still had excellent manners. She was, moreover, mistress of a very pretty little fortune, and was accounted clever without detriment to her amiability, and amiable without detriment to her wit. These facts, as the reader will allow, might have ensured her the very best prospects; but he has seen that she had found herself willing to forfeit her prospects and bury herself in the country. It seemed to her that she had seen enough of the world and of human nature, and that a couple of years of seclusion might not be unprofitable. She had begun to suspect that for a girl of her age she was unduly old and wise— and, what is more, to suspect that others suspected as much. A great observer of life and manners, so far as her opportunities went, she conceived that it behooved her to organize the results of her observation into principles of conduct and of belief. She was becoming—so she argued—too impersonal, too critical, too intelligent, too contemplative, too just. A woman had no business to be so just. The society of nature, of the great expansive skies and the primeval woods, would prove severely unpropitious to her excessive intellectual growth. She would spend her time in the fields and live in her feelings, her simple sense, and the perusal of profitable books from Herbert's library.

She found her brother very prettily housed at about a mile's distance from the nearest town, and at about six miles' distance from another town, the seat of a small college, before which he delivered a weekly lecture. She had seen so little of him of late years that his acquaintance was almost to make; but it was very soon made. Herbert Moore was one of the simplest and least aggressive of men, and one of the most patient and delicate of students. He had a vague notion that Adela was a young woman of extravagant pleasures, and that, somehow, on her arrival, his house would be overrun with the train of her attendant revellers. It was not until after they had been six months together that he discovered that his sister was a model of diligence and temperance. By the time six months more had passed, Adela had bought back a delightful sense of youth and *naïveté*. She learned, under her brother's tuition, to walk—nay, to climb, for there were great hills in the neighborhood—to ride and to botanize. At the end of a year, in the month of August, she received a visit from an old friend, a girl of her own age, who had been spending July at a watering-place, and who was about to be married. Adela had begun to fear that she had lapsed into an almost irreclaimable rusticity, and had suffered a permanent diminution of the social facility for which she had formerly been distinguished; but a week spent in *tête-à-tête* with her friend convinced her not only that she had not forgotten much that she had feared, but also that she had not forgotten much that she had hoped. For this, and other reasons, her friend's departure left her slightly depressed. She felt lonely and even a little elderly. She had lost another illusion. Laura B., for whom a year ago she had entertained a serious regard, now impressed her as a very flimsy little person, who talked about her lover with almost indecent flippancy.

Meanwhile, September was slowly running its course. One morning Mr. Moore took a hasty breakfast and started to catch the train for S., whither a scientific conference called him, which might, he said, release him that afternoon in time for dinner at home, and might, on the other hand, detain him until the evening. It was almost the first time during Adela's rustication that she had been left alone for several hours. Her brother's quiet presence was inappreciable enough; yet now that he was at a distance she nevertheless felt a singular sense of freedom; a sort of return of those days of

early childhood, when, through some domestic catastrophe, she had for an infinite morning been left
to her own devices. What should she do? she asked
herself, half laughing. It was a fair day for work:
but it was a still better one for play. Should she
drive into town and pay a long-standing debt of
morning calls? Should she go into the kitchen and
try her hand at a pudding for dinner? She felt a
delicious longing to do something illicit, to play
with fire, to discover some Bluebeard's closet. But
poor Herbert was no Bluebeard. If she were to
burn down his house he would exact no amends.
Adela went out to the veranda, and, sitting down
on the steps, gazed across the country. It was apparently the last day of Summer. The sky was
faintly blue; the woody hills were putting on the
morbid colors of Autumn; the great pine grove behind the house seemed to have caught and impris-
oned the protesting breezes. Looking down the road
toward the village, it occurred to Adela that she
might have a visit, and so kindly was her mood that
she felt herself competent to a chat with one of her
rustic neighbors. As the sun rose higher, she went
in and established herself with a piece of embroid-
ery in a deep, bow window in the second story,
which, betwixt its muslin curtains and its external
frame-work of vines, commanded most insidiously
the principal approach to the house. While she

drew her threads, she surveyed the road with a deepening conviction that she was destined to have a caller. The air was warm, yet not hot; the dust had been laid during the night by a gentle rain. It had been from the first a source of complaint among Adela's new friends that her courtesies were so thoroughly indiscriminating. Not only had she lent herself to no friendships, but she had committed herself to no preferences. Nevertheless, it was with a by no means impartial fancy that she sat thus expectant at her casement. She had very soon made up her mind that, to answer the exactions of the hour, her visitor should perforce be of the other sex, and as, thanks to the somewhat uncompromising indifference which, during her residence, she had exhibited to the *jeunesse dorée* of the county, her roll-call, in this her hour of need, was limited to a single name, so her thoughts were now centered upon the bearer of that name, Mr. Madison Perkins, the Unitarian minister. If, instead of being Miss Moore's story, this were Mr. Perkins's, it might easily be condensed into the one pregnant fact that he was very far gone in love for our heroine. Although of a different faith from his, she had been so well pleased with one of his sermons, to which she had allowed herself to lend a tolerant ear, that, meeting him some time afterward, she had received him with what she considered a rather knotty doctrinal question; whereupon, gracefully waiving the question, he had asked permission to call upon her and talk over her "difficulties." This short interview had enshrined her in the young minister's heart; and the half-dozen occasions on which he had subsequently contrived to see her had each contributed an additional taper to her shrine. It is but fair to add, however, that, although a captive, Mr. Perkins was as yet no captor. He was simply an honorable young man, who happened at this moment to be the most sympathetic companion within reach. Adela, at twenty-five years of age, had both a past and a future. Mr. Perkins reëchoed the one, and foreshadowed the other.

So, at last, when, as the morning waned toward noon, Adela descried in the distance a man's figure treading the grassy margin of the road, and swinging his stick a she came, she smiled to herself with some complacency. But even while she smiled she became conscious of a most foolish acceleration of the process of her heart. She rose, and resenting her gratuitous emotion, stood for a moment half resolved to have herself denied. As she did so, she glanced along the road again. Her friend had drawn nearer, and, as the distance lessened, lo! it seemed to her that he was not her friend. Before many moments her doubts were removed. The gentleman was a stranger. In front of the house three roads diverged from a great spreading elm. The stranger came along the opposite side of the highway, and when he reached the elm stopped and looked about him as if to verify a direction. Then he deliberately crossed over. Adela had time to see, unseen, that he was a shapely young man, with a bearded chin and a straw hat. After the due interval, Becky, the maid, came up with a card somewhat rudely superscribed in pencil:

> THOMAS LUDLOW,
> *New York.*

Turning it over in her fingers, Adela saw that the reverse of a card had been used, abstracted from the basket on her own drawing-room table. The printed name on the other side was dashed out; it ran: *Mr. Madison Perkins.*

"He asked me to give you this, ma'am," said Becky. "He helped himself to it out of the tray."

"Did he ask for me by name?"

"No, ma'am, he asked for Mr. Moore. When I told him Mr. Moore was away, he asked for some of the family. I told him you were all the family, ma'am."

"Very well," said Adela, "I will go down." But, begging her pardon, we will precede her by a few steps.

Tom Ludlow, as his friends called him, was a

young man of twenty-eight, concerning whom you might have heard the most various opinions; for, as far as he was known (which, indeed, was not very far), he was at once one of the best liked and one of the best hated of men. Born in one of the lower *strata* of New York society, he was still slightly incrusted, if we may so express it, with his native soil. A certain crudity of manners and of aspect proved him to be one of the great majority of the ungloved. On this basis, however, he was a sufficiently good-looking fellow: a middle-sized, agile figure; a head so well shaped as to be handsome; a pair of inquisitive, responsive eyes, and a large, manly mouth, constituting his heritage of beauty. Turned upon the world at an early age, he had, in the pursuit of a subsistence, tried his head at everything in succession, and had generally found it to be quite as hard as the opposing substance; and his figure may have been thought to reflect this sweet assurance in a look of somewhat aggressive satisfaction with things in general, himself included. He was a man of strong faculties and a strong will, but it is doubtful whether his feelings were stronger than he. He was liked for his directness, his good humor, his general soundness and serviceableness; he was disliked for the same qualities under different names; that is, for his impudence, his offensive optimisms, and his inhuman avidity for facts. When his friends insisted upon his noble disinterestedness, his enemies were wont to reply it was all very well to ignore, to nullify oneself in the pursuit of science, but that to suppress the rest of mankind coincidentally betrayed an excess of zeal. Fortunately for Ludlow, on the whole, he was no great listener; and even if he had been, a certain plebeian thick-skinnedness would have been the guaranty of his equanimity; although it must be added that, if, like a genuine democrat, he was very insensitive, like a genuine democrat, too, he was amazingly proud. His tastes, which had always been for the natural sciences, had recently led him to paleontology, that branch of them cultivated by Herbert Moore; and it was upon business connected with this pursuit that, after a short correspondence, he had now come to see him.

As Adela went in to him, he came out with a bow from the window, whence he had been contemplating the lawn. She acknowledged his greeting.

"Miss Moore, I believe," said Ludlow.

"Miss Moore," said Adela.

"I beg your pardon for this intrusion, but as I had come from a distance to see Mr. Moore on business, I thought I might venture either to ask at headquarters how he may most easily be reached, or even to charge you with a message." These words were accompanied with a smile before which it was Adela's destiny to succumb—if this is not too forcible a term for the movement of feeling with which she answered them.

"Pray make no apologies," she said. "We hardly recognize such a thing as intrusion in the country. Won't you sit down? My brother went away only this morning, and I expect him back this afternoon."

"This afternoon? indeed. In that case I believe I'll wait. It was very stupied of me not to have dropped a word beforehand. But I have been in the city all Summer long, and I shall not be sorry to screw a little vacation out of this business. I'm prodigiously fond of the country, and I very seldom get a glimpse of it."

"It's possible," said Adela, "that my brother may not come home until the evening. He was uncertain. You might go to him at S."

Ludlow reflected a moment, with his eyes on his hostess. "If he does return in the afternoon, at what hour will he arrive?"

"At three."

"And my own train leaves at four. Allow him a quarter of an hour to come from town and myself a quarter of an hour to get there (if he would give me his vehicle, back), I should have half an hour to see him. We couldn't do much talk, but I could ask him the essential questions. I wish chiefly to ask him for some letters. It seems a pity to take two superfluous—that is, possibly superfluous—railway journeys of an hour apiece, for I should probably come back with him. Don't you think so?" he asked, very frankly.

"You know best," said Adela. "I'm not particularly fond of the journey to S., even when it's absolutely necessary."

"Yes; and then this is such a lovely day for a good long ramble in the fields. That's a thing I haven't done since I don't know when. I'll stay." And he placed his hat on the floor beside him.

"I'm afraid, now that I think of it," said Adela, "that there is no train until so late an hour that you would have very little time left on your arrival to talk with my brother before the hour at which he himself might have determined to start for home. It's true that you might induce him to remain till the evening."

"Dear me! I shouldn't like to do that. It might be very inconvenient for him. Besides I shouldn't have time. And then I always like to see a man in his own home—or in my own home; a man, that is, whom I have any regard for—and I have a very great regard for your brother, Miss Moore. When men meet at a half-way house, neither feels at his ease. And then this is such an uncommonly pretty place of yours," pursued Ludlow, looking about him.

"Yes, it's a very pretty place," said Adela.

Ludlow got up and walked to the window. "I want to look at your view," said he. "A lovely view it is. You're a happy woman, Miss Moore, to live before such a prospect."

"Yes, if pretty scenery can make one happy, I ought to be happy." And Adela was glad to regain her feet and stand on the other side of the table, before the window.

"Don't you think it can?" asked Ludlow turning around. "I don't know, though, perhaps it can't. Ugly sights can't make you unhappy, necessarily. I've been working for a year in one of the narrowest, darkest, dirtiest, and busiest streets in New York, with rusty bricks and muddy gutters for scenery. But I think I can hardly set up to be miserable. I wish I could. It might be a claim on your favor." As he said these words, he stood leaning against the window shutter, without the curtain, with folded arms. The morning light covered his face, and, mingled with that of his broad laugh, showed Adela that it was a very pleasant face.

"Whatever else he may be," she said to herself as she stood within the shade of the other curtain, playing with the paper-knife which she had plucked from the table. "I think he is honest. I am afraid he isn't a gentleman—but he is not a simpleton."

She met his eye frankly for a moment. "What do you want of my favor?" she asked, with an abruptness of which she was acutely conscious. "Does he wish to make friends," she pursued, "or does he merely wish to pay me a vulgar compliment? There is bad taste, perhaps, in either case, but especially in the latter." Meanwhile her visitor had already answered her.

"What do I want of your favor? Why, I want to make the most of it." And Ludlow blushed at his own audacity.

Adela, however, kept her color. "I'm afraid it will need all your pulling and stretching," she said, with a little laugh.

"All right. I'm great at pulling and stretching," said Ludlow, with a deepening of his great masculine blush, and a broad laugh to match it.

Adela glanced toward the clock on the mantle. She was curious to measure the duration of her acquaintance with this breezy invader of her privacy, with whom she so suddenly found herself bandying florid personalities. She had known him some eight minutes.

Ludlow observed her movement. "I'm interrupting you and detaining you from your own affairs," he said; and he moved toward his hat. "I suppose I must bid you good-morning." And he picked it up.

Adela stood at the table and watched him cross the room. To express a very delicate feeling in terms comparatively broad, she was loth to have him go. She divined, too, that he was loth to go. The knowledge of this feeling on his part, however, affected her composure but slightly. The truth is— we say it with all respect—Adela was an old hand. She was modest, honest and wise; but, as we have said, she had a past—a past of which importunate swains in the guise of morning-callers had been no inconsiderable part; and a great dexterity in what may be called outflanking these gentlemen, was one of her registered accomplishements. Her liveliest emotion at present, therefore, was less one of annoy-ance at her companion than of surprise at her own gracious impulses, which were yet undeniable. "Am I dreaming?" she asked herself. She looked out of the window, and then back at Ludlow, who stood grasping his hat and stick, contemplating her face. Should she bid him remain? "He is honest," she repeated; "why should not I be honest for once?" "I'm sorry you are in a hurry," she said aloud.

"I am in no hurry," he answered.

Adela turned her face to the window again, and toward the opposite hills. There was a moment's pause.

"I thought you were in a hurry," said Ludlow.

Adela gave him her eyes. "My brother would be very glad to have you remain as long as you like. He would expect me to offer you what little hospitality is in my power."

"Pray, offer it then."

"That's easily done. This is the parlor, and there, beyond the hall, is my brother's study. Perhaps you would like to look at his books and his collections. I know nothing about them, and I should be a very poor guide. But you are welcome to go in and use your discretion in examining what may interest you."

"This, I take it, would be but another way of bidding you good-morning."

"For the present, yes."

"But I hesitate to take such liberties with your brother's treasures as you prescribe."

"Prescribe, sir? I prescribe nothing."

"But if I decline to penetrate into Mr. Moore's *sanctum,* what alternative remains?"

"Really—you must make your own alternative."

"I think you mentioned the parlor. Suppose I choose that."

"Just as you please. Here are some books, and, if you like, I will bring you some magazines. Can I serve you in any other way? Are you tired by your walk? Would you like a glass of wine?"

"Tired by my walk?—not exactly. You are very

kind, but I feel no immediate desire for a glass of wine. I think you needn't trouble yourself about the magazines, either. I am in no mood to read. And Ludlow pulled out his watch and compared it with the clock. "I'm afraid your clock is fast."

"Yes;" said Adela, "very likely."

"Some ten minutes. Well, I suppose I had better be walking;" and, coming toward Adela, he extended his hand.

She gave him hers. "It's a day of days for a long, slow ramble," she said.

Ludlow's only rejoinder was his hand-shake. He moved slowly toward the door, half accompanied by Adela. "Poor fellow!" she said to herself. The lattice summer-door admitted into the entry a cool, dusky light, in which Adela looked pale. Ludlow divided its wings with his stick, and disclosed a landscape, long, deep and bright, framed by the pillars of the veranda. He stopped on the threshhold, swinging his stick. "I hope I shan't lose my way," he said.

"I hope not. My brother will not forgive me if you do."

Ludlow's brows were slightly contracted by a frown, but he contrived to smile with his lips. "When shall I come back?" he asked abruptly.

Adela found but a low tone—almost a whisper—

at her command, to answer. ",Whenever you please," she said.

The young man turned about, with his back to the bright doorway, and looked into Adela's face, which was now covered with light. "Miss Moore," said he, "it's very much against my will that I leave you at all."

Adela stood debating within herself. What if her companion should stay? It would, under the circumstances, be an adventure; but was an adventure necessarily unadvisable? It lay wholly with herself to decide. She was her own mistress, and she had hitherto been a just mistress. Might she not for once be a generous one? The reader will observe in Adela's meditation the recurrence of this saving clause "for once." It rests upon the simple fact that she had begun the day in a romantic mood. She was prepared to be interested; and now that an interesting phenomenon had presented itself, that it stood before her in vivid human—nay, manly— shape, instinct with reciprocity, was she to close her hand to the liberality of fate? To do so would be to court mischance; for it would involve, more- over, a petty insult to human nature. Was not the man before her fairly redolent of honesty, and was that not enough? He was not what Adela had been used to call a gentleman. To this conviction she had made a swallow's flight; but from this assurance

she would start. "I have seen" (she thus concluded) "all the gentlemen can show me; let us try something new."

"I see no reason why you should run away so
fast, Mr. Ludlow," she said, aloud.

"I think," cried Ludlow, "it would be the greatest
piece of folly I ever committed."

"I think it would be a pity," said Adela, with a
smile.

"And you invite me into your parlor again? I
come as your visitor, you know. I was your
brother's before. It's a simple enough matter. We
are old friends. We have a broad, common ground
in your brother. Isn't that about it?"

"You may adopt whatever theory you please.
To my mind, it is, indeed, a very simple matter."

"Oh, but I wouldn't have it too simple," said Ludlow, with a mighty smile.

"Have it as you please."

Ludlow leaned back against the doorway. "Your
kindness is too much for me, Miss Moore," said he.
"I am passive; I am in your hands; do with me what
you please. I can't help contrasting my fate with
what it might have been but for you. A quarter of
an hour ago I was ignorant of your existence; you
weren't in my programme. I had no idea your
brother had a sister. When your servant spoke of
'Miss Moore,' upon my word I expected something

rather elderly—something venerable—some rigid old lady, who would say, 'exactly,' and 'very well, sir,' and leave me to spend the rest of the morning tilting back in a chair on the hotel piazza. It shows what fools we are to attempt to forecast the future.

"We must not let our imagination run away with us in any direction," said Adela.

"Imagination? I don't believe I have any. No, madam," and Ludlow straightened himself up, "I live in the present. I write my programme from hour to hour—or, at any rate, I will in the future."

"I think you are very wise," said Adela. "Suppose you write a programme for the present hour. What shall we do? It seems to me a pity to spend so lovely a morning in-doors. I fancy this is the last day of Summer. We ought to celebrate it. How would you like a walk?" Adela had decided that, to reconcile her favors with the proper maintenance of her dignity, her only course was to play the perfect hostess. This decision made, very naturally and gracefully she played her part. It was the one possible part. And yet it did not preclude those delicate sensations with which her novel episode seemed charged: it simply legitimated them. A romantic adventure on so classical a basis would assuredly hurt no one.

"I should like a walk very much," said Ludlow; "a walk with a halt at the end of it."

"Well, if you will consent to a short halt at the beginning of it," said Adela, "I will be with you in a very few minutes." When she returned in her little hat and shawl, she found her friend seated on the veranda steps. He arose and gave her a card.

"I have been requested, in your absence, to hand you this," he said.

Adela read with some compunction the name of Mr. Madison Perkins.

"Has he been here?" she asked. "Why didn't he come in?"

"I told him you were not at home. If it wasn't true then, it was going to be true so soon that the interval was hardly worth taking account of. He addressed himself to me, as I seemed from my position to be quite at home here; but I confess he looked at me as if he doubted my word. He hesitated as to whether he should confide his name to me, or whether he should confide it in that shape to the entry table. I think he wished to show me that he suspected my veracity, for he was making rather grimly for the table when I, fearing that once inside the house he might encounter the living truth, informed him in the most good-humored tone possible that I would take charge of his little tribute."

"I think, Mr. Ludlow, that you are a strangely unscrupulous man. How did you know that Mr. Perkins's business was not urgent?"

"I didn't know it. But I knew it could be no more urgent than mine. Depend upon it, Miss Moore, you have no case against me. I only pretend to be a man; to have admitted that charming young gentleman would have been heroic."

Adela was familiar with a sequestered spot, in the very heart of the fields, as it seemed to her, to which she now proposed to conduct her friend. The point was to select a goal neither too distant nor too near, and to adopt a pace neither too rapid nor too slow. But although Adela's happy valley was a good two miles away, and they had measured the interval with the very *minimum* of speed, yet most sudden seemed their arrival at the stile over which Adela was used to strike into the meadows. Once on the road, she felt a precipitate conviction that there could be no evil in an adventure so essentially wholesome as that to which she had lent herself, and that there could be no guile in a spirit so deeply sensitive to the sacred influences of Nature, and to the melancholy aspect of incipient Autumn as that of her companion. A man with an unaffected relish for small children is a man to inspire young women with a generouse confidence; and so, in a lesser degree, a man with a genuine feeling for the simple beauties of a common New England landscape may not unreasonably be accepted by the daughters of the scene as a person worthy of their esteem. Adela was a great observer of the clouds, the trees and the streams, the sounds and colors, the echoes and reflections native to her adopted home; and she experienced an honest joy at the sight of Ludlow's keen appreciation of these modest facts. His enjoyment of them, deep as it was, however, had to struggle against that sensuous depression natural to a man who has spent the Summer in a close and fetid laboratory in the heart of a great city, and against a sensation of a less material color—the feeling that Adela was a delightful girl. Still, naturally a great talker, he celebrated his impressions in a generous flow of good-humored eloquence. Adela resolved within herself that he was decidedly a companion for the open air. He was a man to make use, even to abuse, of the wide horizon and the high ceiling of Nature. The freedom of his gestures, the sonority of his voice, the keenness of his vision, the general vivacity of his manners, seemed to necessitate and to justify a universal absence of barriers. They crossed the stile, and waded through the long grass of several successive meadows, until the ground began to rise, the stony surfaces to crop through the turf, when, after a short ascent, they reached a broad plateau, covered with boulders and shrubs, which lost itself on one side in a short, steep cliff, whence fields and marshes stretched down to the opposite river; and on the other, in scattered clumps of pine and maple, which gradually thickened and multiplied, until the horizon in that quarter was blue with a long line of woods. Here was both sun and shade—the unobstructed sky, or the whispering dome of a circle of pines. Adela led the way to a sunny seat among the rocks, which commanded the course of the river, and where a cluster of trees would lend an admonitory undertone to their conversation.

Before long, however, its muffled eloquence became rather importunate, and Adela remarked upon the essential melancholy of the phenomenon.

"It has always seemed to me," rejoined Ludlow, "that the wind in the pines expresses tolerably well man's sense of a coming change, simply *as* a change."

"Perhaps it does," said Adela. "The pines are forever rustling, and men are forever changing."

"Yes, but they can only be said to express it when there is some one there to hear them; and more especially some one in whose life a change is, to his own knowledge, going to take place. Then they are quite prophetic. Don't you know Longfellow says so?"

"Yes, I know Longfellow says so. But you seem to speak from your own feeling."

"I do."

"Is there a change pending in your life?"

"Yes, rather an important one."

"I believe that's what men say when they are going to be married," said Adela.

"I'm going to be divorced, rather. I'm going to Europe."

"Indeed! soon?"

"To-morrow," said Ludlow, after an instant's pause.

"Oh!" said Adela. "How I envy you!"

Ludlow. who sat looking over the cliff and tossing stones down into the plain, observed a certain inequality in the tone of his companion's two exclamations. The first was nature, the second art. He turned his eyes upon her, but she had turned hers away upon the distance. Then, for a moment, he retreated within himself and thought. He rapidly surveyed his position. Here was he, Tom Ludlow, a hard-headed son of toil, without fortune, without credit, without antecedents, whose lot was cast exclusively with vulgar males, and who had never had a mother, a sister nor a well-bred sweetheart to pitch his voice for the feminine tympanum; who had seldom come nearer an indubitable young lady than, in a favoring crowd, to receive a mechanical "thank you" (as if he were a policeman), for some ingeniously provoked service; here he found himself up to his neck in a sudden pastoral with the most ladyish young woman in the land. That it was in him to enjoy the society of such a woman (provided, of course, she were not a fool), he very well knew; but he had not yet suspected that it was possible for him (in the midst of more serious cares) to obtain it. Was he now to infer that this final gift was his—the gift of pleasing women who were worth the pleasing? The inference was at least logical. He had made a good impression. Why else should a modest and discerning girl have so speedily granted him her favor? It was with a little thrill of satisfaction that Ludlow reflected upon the directness of his course. "It all comes back," he said to himself, "to my old theory, that a process can't be too simple. I used no arts. In such an enterprise I shouldn't have known where to begin. It was my ignorance of the regulation method that served me. Women like a gentleman, of course; but they like a man better." It was the little touch of nature he had discerned in Adela's tone that had set him thinking; but as compared with the frankness of his own attitude it betrayed after all no undue emotion. Ludlow had accepted the fact of his adaptability to the idle mood of a cultivated woman in a thoroughly rational spirit, and he was not now tempted to exaggerate its bearings. He was not the man to be intoxicated by success— this or any other. "If Miss Moore," he pursued, "is so wise—or so foolish—as to like me half an hour for what I am, she is welcome. Assuredly," he added, as he gazed at her intelligent profile, "she will not like me for what I am not." It needs a woman, however, far more intelligent than (thank heaven!) most women are—more intelligent, certainly, than Adela was—to guard her happiness against a strong man's consistent assumption of her intelligence; and doubtless it was from a sense of this general truth, as Ludlow still gazed, he felt an emotion of manly tenderness. "I wouldn't offend her for the world," he thought. Just then, Adela, conscious of his gaze, looked about; and before he knew it, Ludlow had repeated aloud, "Miss Moore, I wouldn't offend you for the world."

Adela glanced at him for a moment with a little flush that subsided into a smile. "To what dreadful injury is that the prelude?" she asked.

"It's the prelude to nothing. It refers to the past —to any possible displeasure I may have caused you."

"Your scruples are unnecessary, Mr. Ludlow. If you had given me offence, I should not have left you to apologize for it. I should not have left the matter to occur to you as you sat dreaming charitably in the sun."

"What would you have done?"

"Done? nothing. You don't imagine I would have rebuked you—or snubbed you—or answered

you back, I take it. I would have left undone—
what, I can't tell you. Ask yourself what I have
done. I'm sure I hardly know myself," said Adela,
with some intensity. "At all events, here I am
sitting with you in the fields, as if you were a friend
of years. Why do you speak of offence?" And
Adela (an uncommon accident with her) lost command of her voice, which trembled ever so slightly.
"What an odd thought! why should you offend
me? Do I invite it?" Her color had deepened
again, and her eyes brightened. She had forgotten
herself, and before speaking had not, as was her
wont, sought counsel of that staunch conservative,
her taste. She had spoken from a full heart—a
heart which had been filling rapidly since the outset
of their walk with a feeling almost passionate in its
quality, and which that little blast of prose which
had brought her Ludlow's announcement of his departure, had caused to overflow. The reader may
give this feeling such a name as he pleases. We will
content ourselves with saying that Adela had played with fire so effectually that she had been scorched.
The slight vehemence of the speech just quoted had
covered her sensation of pain.

"You pull one up rather short, Miss Moore,"
said Ludlow. "A man says the best he can."

Adela made no reply. For a moment she hung
her head. Was she to cry out because she was hurt?

Was she to introduce her injured soul as an impertinent third into the company? No! Here our reserved and contemplative heroine is herself again.
Her part was still to be the perfect young lady. For
our own part, we can imagine no figure more be-
witching than that of the perfect young lady under
these circumstances; and if Adela had been the most
accomplished coquette in the world she could not
have assumed a more becoming expression than the
air of languid equanimity which now covered her
features. But having paid this generous homage to
propriety, she felt free to suffer. Raising her eyes
from the ground, she abruptly addressed her companion with this injunction:

"Mr. Ludlow," said she, "tell me something about
yourself."

Ludlow burst into a laugh. "What shall I tell
you?"

"Everything."

"Everything? Excuse me, I'm not such a fool.
But do you know that's a delicious request you
make? I suppose I ought to blush and hesitate;
but I never yet blushed or hesitated in the right
place."

"Very good. There is one fact. Continue. Begin at the beginning."

"Well, let me see. My name you know. I'm
twenty-eight years old."

"That's the end," said Adela.

"But you don't want the history of my babyhood, I take it. I imagine that I was a very big, noisy and ugly baby: what's called a 'splendid infant.' My parents were poor, and, of course, honest. They belonged to a very different set—or 'sphere', I suppose you call it—from any you probably know. They were working people. My father was a chemist in a small way, and I fancy my mother was not above using her hands to turn a penny. But although I don't remember her, I am sure she was a good, sound woman; I feel her occasionally in my own sinews. I myself have been at work all my life, and a very good worker I am, let me tell you. I'm not patient, as I imagine your brother to be—although I have more patience than you might suppose—but I'm plucky. If you think I'm over-egotistical, remember 'twas you began it. I don't know whether I'm clever, and I don't much care; that word is used only by unpractical people. But I'm clear-headed, and inquisitive, and enthusiastic. That's as far as I can describe myself. I don't know anything about my character. I simply suspect I'm a pretty good fellow. I don't know whether I'm grave or gay, lively or severe. I don't know whether I'm high-tempered or low-tempered. I don't believe I'm 'high-toned.' I fancy I'm good-natured enough, inasmuch as I'm not nervous. I should not be at all surprised to discover I was prodigiously conceited; but I'm afraid the discovery wouldn't cut me down, much. I'm desperately hard to snub, I know. Oh, you would think me a great brute if you knew me. I should hesitate to say whether I am of a loving turn. I know I'm desperately tired of a number of persons who are very fond of me; I'm afraid I'm ungrateful. Of course as a man speaking to a woman, there's nothing for it but to say I'm selfish; but I hate to talk about such windy abstractions. In the way of positive facts: I'm not educated. I know no Greek and very little Latin. But I can honestly say that first and last I have read a great many books—and, thank God, I have a memory! And I have some tastes, too. I'm very fond of music. I have a good old voice of my own: *that* I can't help knowing; and I'm not one to be bullied about pictures. Is that enough? I'm conscious of an utter inability to say anything to the point. To put myself in a nutshell, I suppose I'm simply a working man; I have his virtues and I have his defects. I'm a very common fellow."

"Do you call yourself a very common fellow because you really believe yourself to be one, or because you are weakly tempted to disfigure your rather flattering catalogue with a great final blot?"

"I'm sure I don't know. You show more subtlety

in that one question than I have shown in my whole string of affirmations. You women are strong on asking witty questions. Seriously, I believe I *am* a common fellow. I wouldn't make the admission to every one though. But to you, Miss Moore, who sit there under your parasol as impartial as the Muse of History, to you I own the truth. I'm no man of genius. There is something I miss; some final distinction I lack; you may call it what you please. Perhaps it's humility. Perhaps you can find it in Ruskin, somewhere. Perhaps it's patience— perhaps it's imagination. I'm vulgar, Miss Moore. I'm the vulgar son of vulgar people. I use the word, of course, in its strictest sense. So much I grant you at the outset, and then I walk ahead."

"Have you any sisters?"

"Not a sister; and no brothers, nor cousins, nor uncles, nor aunts."

"And you sail for Europe to-morrow?"

"To-morrow, at ten o'clock."

"To be away how long?"

"As long as I possibly can. Five years if possible."

"What do you expect to do in those five years?"

"Study."

"Nothing but study?"

"It will all come back to that, I fancy. I hope to enjoy myself reasonably, and to look at the world as I go. But I must not waste time; I'm growing old."

"Where are you going?"

"To Berlin. I wanted to get letters from your brother."

"Have you money? Are you well off?"

"Well off? Not I, no. I'm poor. I travel on a little money that has just come to me from an unexpected quarter: an old debt owing my father. It will take me to Germany and keep me for six months. After that I shall work my way."

"Are you happy? Are you contented?"

"Just now I'm pretty comfortable, thank you."

"But will you be so when you get to Berlin?"

"I don't promise to be contented; but I'm pretty sure to be happy."

"Well!" said Adela, "I sincerely hope you may be."

"Amen!" said Ludlow.

Of what more was said at this moment, no record may be given. The reader has been put into possession of the key of our friends' conversation; it is only needful to say that substantially upon this key, it was prolonged for half an hour more. As the minutes elapsed, Adela found herself drifting further and further away from her anchorage. When at last she compelled herself to consult her watch, and remind her companion that there remained but just time enough for them to reach home, in anticipation of her brother's arrival, she knew that she was rapidly floating seaward. As she descended the hill at her companion's side, she felt herself suddenly thrilled by an acute temptation. Her first instinct was to close her eyes upon it, in the trust that when she opened them again it would have vanished; but she found that it was not to be so uncompromisingly dismissed. It importuned her so effectually, that before she had walked a mile homeward, she had succumbed to it, or had at least given it the pledge of that quickening of the heart which accompanies a bold resolution. This little sacrifice allowed her no breath for idle words, and she accordingly advanced with a bent and listening head. Ludlow marched along, with no apparent diminution of his habitual buoyancy of mien, talking as fast and as loud as at the outset. He adventured a prophecy that Mr. Moore would not have returned, and charged Adela with a humorous message of regrets. Adela had begun by wondering whether the approach of their separation had wrought within him any sentimental depression at all commensurate with her own, with that which sealed her lips and weighed upon her heart; and now she was debating as to whether his express declaration that he felt "awfully blue" ought necessarily to remove her doubts. Ludlow followed up this declaration with a very pretty review of the morning, and a sober valedictory which, whether intensely felt or not, struck Adela as at least nobly bare of flimsy compliments. He might be a common fellow—but he was certainly a very uncommon one. When they reached the garden gate, it was with a fluttering heart that Adela scanned the premises for some accidental sign of her brother's presence. She felt that there would be an especial fitness in his not having returned. She led the way in. The hall table was bare of his hat and overcoat. The only object it displayed was Mr. Perkins's card, which Adela had deposited there on her exit. All that was represented by that little white ticket seemed a thousand miles away. Finally, Mr. Moore's absence from his study was conclusive against his return.

As Adela went back thence into the drawing-room, she simply shook her head at Ludlow, who was standing before the fire-place; and as she did so, she caught her reflection in the mantel-glass. "Verily," she said to herself, "I have travelled far." She had pretty well unlearned the repose of the Veres of Vere. But she was to break with it still more completely. It was with a singular hardihood that she prepared to redeem the little pledge which had been extorted from her on her way home. She felt that there was no trial to which her generosity might now be called which she would not hail with enthusiasm. Unfortunately, her generosity was not likely to be challenged; although she nevertheless had the satisfaction of assuring herself at this moment that, like the mercy of the Lord, it was infinite. Should she satisfy herself of her friend's? or should she leave it delightfully uncertain? These had been the terms of what has been called her temptation, at the foot of the hill. But inasmuch as Adela was by no means strictly engaged in the pursuit of pleasure, and as the notion of a grain of suffering was by no means repugnant to her, she had resolved to obtain possession of the one essential fact of her case, even though she should be at heavy costs to maintain it.

"Well, I have very little time," said Ludlow; "I must get my dinner and pay my bill and drive to the train." And he put out his hand.

Adela gave him her own, and looked him full in the eyes. "You are in a great hurry," said she.

"It's not I who am in a hurry. It's my confounded destiny. It's the train and the steamer."

"If you really wished to stay you wouldn't be bullied by the train and the steamer."

"Very true—very true. But *do* I really wish to stay?"

"That's the question. That's what I want to know."

"You ask difficult questions, Miss Moore."

"I mean they shall be difficult."

"Then, of course, you are prepared to answer difficult ones."

"I don't know that that's of course, but I am."

"Well, then, do you wish me to stay? All I have to do is to throw down my hat, sit down and fold my arms for twenty minutes. I lose my train and my ship. I stay in America, instead of going to Europe."

"I have thought of all that."

"I don't mean to say it's a great deal. There are pleasures and pleasures."

"Yes, and especially the former. It is a great deal."

"And you invite me to accept it?"

"No; I ought not to say that. What I ask of you is whether, if I should so invite you, you would say 'yes.'"

"That makes the matter very easy for you, Miss Moore. What attractions do you hold out?"

"I hold out nothing whatever, sir."

"I suppose that means a great deal."

"It means what it seems to mean."

"Well, you are certainly a most interesting woman, Miss Moore—a charming woman."

"Why don't you call me 'fascinating' at once, and bid me good morning?"

"I don't know but that I shall have to come to

that. But I will give you no answer that leaves you at an advantage. Ask me to stay—command me to stay, if that suits you better—and I will see how it sounds. Come, you must not trifle with a man." He still held Adela's hand, and they had been looking frankly into each other's eyes. He paused, waiting for an answer.

"Good-by, Mr. Ludlow," said Adela. "God bless you!" And she was about to withdraw her hand; but he held it.

"Are we friends?" said he.

Adela gave a little shrug of her shoulders. "Friends of three hours."

Ludlow looked at her with some sternness. "Our parting could at best hardly have been sweet," said he; "but why should you make it bitter, Miss Moore?"

"If it's bitter, why should you try to change it?"

"Because I don't like bitter things."

Ludlow had caught a glimpse of the truth—that truth of which the reader has had a glimpse—and he stood there at once thrilled and annoyed. He had both a heart and a conscience. "It's not my fault," he cried to the latter; but he was unable to add, in all consistency, that it was his misfortune. It would be very heroic, very poetic, very chivalric, to lose his steamer, and he felt that he could do so for sufficient cause—at the suggestion of a fact. But the motive

here was less than a fact—an idea; less than an idea
—a fancy. "It's a very pretty little romance as it
is," he said to himself. "Why spoil it? She is an
admirable girl: to have learned that is enough for
me." He raised her hand to his lips, pressed them
to it, dropped it, reached the door and bounded out
of the garden gate.

The day was ended.

IV

A MOST EXTRAORDINARY CASE

A MOST EXTRAORDINARY CASE

LATE in the spring of the year 1865, just as the war had come to a close, a young invalid officer lay in bed in one of the uppermost chambers of one of the great New York hotels. His meditations were interrupted by the entrance of a waiter, who handed him a card superscribed *Mrs. Samuel Mason,* and bearing on its reverse the following words in pencil: "Dear Colonel Mason, I have only just heard of your being here, ill and alone. It's too dreadful. Do you remember me? Will you see me? If you do, I think you *will* remember me. I insist on coming up. M. M."

Mason was undressed, unshaven, weak, and feverish. His ugly little hotel chamber was in a state of confusion which had not even the merit of being picturesque. Mrs. Mason's card was at once a puzzle and a heavenly intimation of comfort. But all that it represented was so dim to the young man's enfeebled perception that it took him some moments to collect his thoughts.

"It's a lady, sir," said the waiter, by way of assisting him.

"Is she young or old?" asked Mason.

"Well, sir, she's a little of both."

"I can't ask a lady to come up here," groaned the invalid.

"Upon my word, sir, you look beautiful," said the waiter. "They like a sick man. And I see she's of your own name," continued Michael, in whom constant service had bred great frankness of speech; "the more shame to her for not coming before."

Colonel Mason concluded that, as the visit had been of Mrs. Mason's own seeking, he would receive her without more ado. "If she doesn't mind it, I'm sure I needn't," said the poor fellow, who hadn't the strength to be over-punctilious. So in a very few moments his visitor was ushered up to his bedside. He saw before him a handsome, middle-aged blonde woman, stout of figure, and dressed in the height of the fashion, who displayed no other embarrassment than such as was easily explained by the loss of breath consequent on the ascent of six flights of stairs.

"Do you remember me?" she asked, taking the young man's hand.

He lay back on his pillow, and looked at her. "You used to be my aunt,—my aunt Maria," he said.

"I'm your aunt Maria still," she answered. "It's very good of you not to have forgotten me."

"It's very good of you not to have forgotten *me*," said Mason, in a tone which betrayed a deeper feeling than the wish to return a civil speech.

"Dear me, you've had the war and a hundred dreadful things. I've been living in Europe, you know. Since my return I've been living in the country, in your uncle's old house on the river, of which the lease had just expired when I came home. I came to town yesterday on business, and accidentally heard of your condition and your whereabouts. I knew you'd gone into the army, and I had been wondering a dozen times what had become of you, and whether you wouldn't turn up now that the war's at last over. Of course I didn't lose a moment in coming to you. I'm *so* sorry for you." Mrs. Mason looked about her for a seat. The chairs were encumbered with odds and ends belonging to her nephew's wardrobe and to his equipment, and with the remnants of his last repast. The good lady surveyed the scene with the beautiful mute irony of compassion.

The young man lay watching her comely face in delicious submission to whatever form of utterance this feeling might take. "You're the first woman—to call a woman—I've seen in I don't know how many months," he said, contrasting her appearance with that of his room, and reading her thoughts.

"I should suppose so. I mean to be as good as a dozen. She disembarrassed one of the chairs, and brought it to the bed. Then, seating herself, she ungloved one of her hands, and laid it softly on the young man's wrist. "What a great full-grown young fellow you've become!" she pursued. "Now, tell me, are you very ill?"

"You must ask the doctor," said Mason. "I actually don't know. I'm extremely uncomfortable, but I suppose it's partly my circumstances."

"I've no doubt it's more than half your circumstances. I've seen the doctor. Mrs. Van Zandt is an old friend of mine; and when I come to town, I always go to see her. It was from her I learned this morning that you were here in this state. We had begun by rejoicing over the new prospects of peace; and from that, of course, we had got to lamenting the numbers of young men who are to enter upon it with lost limbs and shattered health. It happened that Mrs. Van Zandt mentioned several of her husband's patients as examples, and yourself among the number. You were an excellent young man, miserably sick, without family or friends, and with no asylum but a suffocating little closet in a noisy hotel. You may imagine that I pricked up my ears, and asked your baptismal name. Dr. Van Zandt came in, and told me. Your name is luckily an uncommon one; it's absurd to suppose that there could be two Ferdinand Masons. In short, I felt that you were my husband's brother's child, and that at last I too might have my little turn at hero-nursing. The little that the Doctor knew of your history agreed with the little that I knew, though I confess I was sorry to hear that you had never spoken of our relationship. But why should you? At all events you've got to acknowledge it now. I regret your not having said something about it before, only because the Doctor might have brought us together a month ago, and you would now have been well."

"It will take me more than a month to get well," said Mason, feeling that, if Mrs. Mason was meaning to exert herself on his behalf, she should know the real state of the case. "I never spoke of you, because I had quite lost sight of you. I fancied you were still in Europe; and indeed," he added, after a moment's hesitation, "I heard that you had married again."

"Of course you did," said Mrs. Mason, placidly. "I used to hear it once a month myself. But I had a much better right to fancy you married. Thank Heaven, however, there's nothing of that sort between us. We can each do as we please. I promise to cure you in a month, in spite of yourself."

"What's your remedy?" asked the young man, with a smile very courteous, considering how sceptical it was.

"My first remedy is to take you out of this horrible hole. I talked it all over with Dr. Van Zandt. He says you must get into the country. Why, my dear boy, this is enough to kill you outright,—one Broadway outside of your window and another outside of your door! Listen to me. My house is directly on the river, and only two hours' journey by rail. You know I've no children. My only companion is my niece, Caroline Hofmann. You shall come and stay with us until you are as strong as you need be,—if it takes a dozen years. You shall have sweet, cool air, and proper food, and decent attendance, and the devotion of a sensible woman. I shall not listen to a word of objection. You shall do as you please, get up when you please, dine when you please, go to bed when you please, and say what you please. I shall ask nothing of you but to let yourself be very dearly cared for. Do you remember how, when you were a boy at school, after your father's death, you were taken with measles, and your uncle had you brought to our own house? I helped to nurse you myself, and I remember what nice manners you had in the very

midst of your measles. Your uncle was very fond
of you; and if he had had any considerable property
of his own, I know he would have remembered you
in his will. But, of course, he couldn't leave away
his wife's money. What I wish to do for you is a
very small part of what he would have done, if he
had only lived, and heard of your gallantry and
your sufferings. So it's settled. I shall go home
this afternoon. To-morrow morning I shall despatch
my man-servant to you with instructions. He's an
Englishman. He thoroughly knows his business,
and he will put up your things, and save you every
particle of trouble. You've only to let yourself be
dressed, and driven to the train. I shall, of course,
meet you at your journey's end. Now don't tell me
you're not strong enough."

"I feel stronger at this moment than I've felt in
a dozen weeks," said Mason. "It's useless for me
to attempt to thank you."

"Quite useless. I shouldn't listen to you. And
I suppose," added Mrs. Mason, looking over the
bare walls and scanty furniture of the room, "you
pay a fabulous price for this bower of bliss. Do you
need money?"

The young man shook his head.

"Very well then," resumed Mrs. Mason, con-
clusively, "from this moment you're in my
hands."

The young man lay speechless from the very fulness of his heart; but he strove by the pressure of his fingers to give her some assurance of his gratitude. His companion rose, and lingered beside him, drawing on her glove, and smiling quietly with the look of a long-baffled philanthropist who has at last discovered a subject of infinite capacity. Poor Ferdinand's weary visage reflected her smile. Finally, after the lapse of years, he too was being cared for. He let his head sink into the pillow, and silently inhaled the perfume of her sober elegance and her cordial good-nature. He felt like taking her dress in his hand, and asking her not to leave him,—now that solitude would be bitter. His eyes, I suppose, betrayed this touching apprehension,— doubly touching in a war-wasted young officer. As she prepared to bid him farewell, Mrs. Mason stooped, and kissed his forehead. He listened to the rustle of her dress across the carpet, to the gentle closing of the door, and to her retreating footsteps. And then, giving way to his weakness, he put his hands to his face, and cried like a homesick schoolboy. He had been reminded of the exquisite side of life.

Matters went forward as Mrs. Mason had arranged them. At six o'clock on the following evening Ferdinand found himself deposited at one of the way stations of the Hudson River Railroad, exhausted by his journey, and yet excited at the prospect of its drawing to a close. Mrs. Mason was in waiting in a low basket-phaeton, with a magazine of cushions and wrappings. Ferdinand transferred himself to her side, and they drove rapidly homeward. Mrs. Mason's house was a cottage of liberal make, with a circular lawn, a sinuous avenue, and a well-grown plantation of shrubbery. As the phaeton drew up before the porch, a young lady appeared in the doorway. Mason will be forgiven if he considered himself presented *ex officio,* as I may say, to this young lady. Before he really knew it, and in the absence of the servant, who, under Mrs. Mason's directions, was busy in the background with his trunk, he had availed himself of her proffered arm, and had allowed her to assist him through the porch, across the hall, and into the parlor, where she graciously consigned him to a sofa which, for his especial use, she had caused to be wheeled up before a fire kindled for his especial comfort. He was unable, however, to take advantage of her good offices. Prudence dictated that without further delay he should betake himself to his room.

On the morning after his arrival he got up early, and made an attempt to be present at breakfast; but his strength failed him, and he was obliged to dress at his leisure, and content himself with a simple transition from his bed to his arm-chair.

The chamber assigned him was designedly on the ground-floor, so that he was spared the trouble of measuring his strength with the staircase,—a charming room, brightly carpeted and upholstered, and marked by a certain fastidious freshness which betrayed the uncontested dominion of women. It had a broad high window, draped in chintz and crisp muslin and opening upon the greensward of the lawn. At this window, wrapped in his dressing-gown, and lost in the embrace of the most unresisting of arm-chairs, he slowly discussed his simple repast. Before long his hostess made her appearance on the lawn outside the window. As this quarter of the house was covered with warm sunshine, Mason ventured to open the window and talk to her, while she stood out on the grass beneath her parasol.

"It's time to think of your physician," she said. "You shall choose for yourself. The great physician here is Dr. Gregory, a gentleman of the old school. We have had him but once, for my niece and I have the health of a couple of dairy-maids. On that one occasion he—well, he made a fool of himself. His practice is among the 'old families,' and he only knows how to treat certain old-fashioned, obsolete complaints. Anything brought about by the war would be quite out of his range. And then he vacillates, and talks about his own maladies *à lui*.

And, to tell the truth, we had a little repartee which makes our relations somewhat ambiguous."

"I see he would never do," said Mason, laughing. "But he's not your only physician?"

"No: there is a young man, a newcomer, a Dr. Knight, whom I don't know, but of whom I've heard very good things. I confess that I have a prejudice in favor of the young men. Dr. Knight has a position to establish, and I suppose he's likely to be especially attentive and careful. I believe, moreover, that he's been an army surgeon."

"I knew a man of his name," said Mason. "I wonder if this is he. His name was Horace Knight, —a light-haired, near-sighted man."

"I don't know," said Mrs. Mason; "perhaps Caroline knows." She retreated a few steps, and called to an upper window: "Caroline, what's Dr. Knight's first name?"

Mason listened to Miss Hofmann's answer,— "I haven't the least idea."

"Is it Horace?"

"I don't know."

"Is he light or dark?"

"I've never seen him."

"Is he near-sighted?"

"How in the world should I know?"

"I fancy he's as good as any one," said Ferdinand.

"With you, my dear aunt, what does the doctor matter?"

Mrs. Mason accordingly sent for Dr. Knight, who, on arrival, turned out to be her nephew's old acquaintance. Although the young men had been united by no greater intimacy than the superficial comradeship resulting from a winter in neighboring quarters, they were very well pleased to come together again. Horace Knight was a young man of good birth, good looks, good faculties, and good intentions, who, after a three years' practice of surgery in the army, had undertaken to push his fortune in Mrs. Mason's neighborhood. His mother, a widow with a small income, had recently removed to the country for economy, and her son had been unwilling to leave her to live alone. The adjacent country, moreover, offered a promising field for a man of energy,—a field well stocked with large families of easy income and of those conservative habits which lead people to make much of the cares of a physician. The local practitioner had survived the glory of his prime, and was not, perhaps, entirely guiltless of Mrs. Mason's charge, that he had not kept up with the progress of the "new diseases." The world, in fact, was getting too new for him, as well as for his old patients. He had had money invested in the South,—precious sources of revenue, which the war had swallowed up at a gulp; he had grown frightened and nervous and querulous; he had lost his presence of mind and his spectacles in several important conjunctures; he had been repeatedly and distinctly fallible; a vague dissatisfaction pervaded the breasts of his patrons; he was without competitors: in short, fortune was propitious to Dr. Knight. Mason remembered the young physician only as a good-humored, intelligent companion; but he soon had reason to believe that his medical skill would leave nothing to be desired. He arrived rapidly at a clear understanding of Ferdinand's case; he asked intelligent questions, and gave simple and definite instructions. The disorder was deeply seated and virulent, but there was no apparent reason why unflinching care and prudence should not subdue it.

"Your strength is very much reduced," he said, as he took his hat and gloves to go; "but I should say you had an excellent constitution. It seems to me, however,—if you will pardon me for saying so, —to be partly your own fault that you have fallen so low. You have opposed no resistance; you haven't cared to get well."

"I confess that I haven't,—particularly. But I don't see how you should know it."

"Why it's obvious."

"Well, it was natural enough. Until Mrs. Mason discovered me, I hadn't a friend in the world. I had become demoralized by solitude. I had almost forgotten the difference between sickness and health. I had nothing before my eyes to remind me in tangible form of that great mass of common human interests for the sake of which—under whatever name he may disguise the impulse—a man continues in health and recovers from disease. I had forgotten that I ever cared for books or ideas, or anything but the preservation of my miserable carcass. My carcass had become quite too miserable to be an object worth living for. I was losing time and money at an appalling rate; I was getting worse rather than better; and I therefore gave up resistance. It seemed better to die easy than to die hard. I put it all in the past tense, because within these three days I've become quite another man."

"I wish to Heaven I could have heard of you," said Knight. "I would have made you come home with me, if I could have done nothing else. It was certainly not a rose-colored prospect; but what do you say now?" he continued, looking around the room. "I should say that at the present moment rose-color was the prevailing hue."

Mason assented with an eloquent smile.

"I congratulate you from my heart. Mrs. Mason —if you don't mind my speaking of her—is so thoroughly (and, I should suppose, incorrigibly) good-natured, that it's quite a surprise to find her extremely sensible."

"Yes; and so resolute and sensible in her better moments," said Ferdinand, "that it's quite a surprise to find her good-natured. She's a fine woman."

"But I should say that your especial blessing was your servant. He looks as if he had come out of an English novel."

"My especial blessing! You haven't seen Miss Hofmann, then?"

"Yes: I met her in the hall. She looks as if she had come out of an American novel. I don't know that that's great praise; but, at all events, I make her come out of it."

"You're bound in honor, then," said Mason, laughing, "to put her into another."

Mason's conviction of his newly made happiness needed no enforcement at the Doctor's hands. He felt that it would be his own fault if these were not among the most delightful days of his life. He resolved to give himself up without stint to his impressions,—utterly to vegetate. His illness alone would have been a sufficient excuse for a long term of intellectual laxity; but Mason had other good reasons besides. For the past three years he had been stretched without intermission on the rack of duty. Although constantly exposed to hard service, it had been his fortune never to receive a serious

wound; and, until his health broke down, he had
taken fewer holidays than any officer I ever heard
of. With an abundance of a certain kind of equanimity and self-control,—a faculty of ready self-
adaptation to the accomplished fact, in any direction,—he was yet in his innermost soul a singularly
nervous, over-scrupulous person. On the few occasions when he had been absent from the scene of his
military duties, although duly authorized and war-
ranted in the act, he had suffered so acutely from
the apprehension that something was happening, or
was about to happen, which not to have witnessed
or to have had a hand in would be matter of eternal
mortification, that he can be barely said to have
enjoyed his recreation. The sense of lost time was,
moreover, his perpetual bugbear,—the feeling that
precious hours were now fleeting uncounted, which
in more congenial labors would suffice almost for the
building of a monument more lasting than brass.
This feeling he strove to propitiate as much as possible by assiduous reading and study in the interval
of his actual occupations. I cite the fact merely
as an evidence of the uninterrupted austerity of his
life for a long time before he fell sick. I might
triple this period, indeed, by a glance at his college
years, and at certain busy months which intervened
between this close of his youth and the opening of
the war. Mason had always worked. He was fond

of work to begin with; and, in addition, the complete absence of family ties had allowed him to follow his tastes without obstruction or diversion. This circumstance had been at once a great gain to him and a serious loss. He reached his twenty-seventh year a very accomplished scholar, as scholars go, but a great dunce in certain social matters. He was quite ignorant of all those lighter, more evanescent forms of conviviality attached to being somebody's son, brother, or cousin. At last, however, as he reminded himself, he was to discover what it was to be the nephew of somebody's husband. Mrs. Mason was to teach him the meaning of the adjective *domestic*. It would have been hard to learn it in a pleasanter way. Mason felt that he was to learn something from his very idleness, and that he would leave the house a wiser as well as a better man. It became probable, thanks to that quickening of the faculties which accompanies the dawning of a sincere and rational attachment, that in this last respect he would not be disappointed. Very few days sufficed to reveal to him the many excellent qualities of his hostess,—her warm capacious heart, her fairness of mind, her good temper, her good taste, her vast fund of experience and of reminiscence, and, indeed, more than all, a certain passionate devotedness, to which fortune, in leaving her a childless widow, had done but scant justice. The two accordingly established a friendship,—a friendship that promised as well for the happiness of each as any that ever undertook to meddle with happiness. If I were telling my story from Mrs. Mason's point of view, I take it that I might make a very good thing of the statement that this lady had deliberately and solemnly conferred her affection upon my hero; but I am compelled to let it stand in this simple shape. Excellent, charming person that she was, she had every right to the rich satisfaction which belonged to a liberal—yet not too liberal—estimate of her guest. She had divined him,—so much the better for her. That it was very much the better for him is obviously one of the elementary facts of my narrative; a fact of which Mason became so rapidly and profoundly sensible, that he was soon able to dismiss it from his thoughts to his life,—its proper sphere.

In the space of ten days, then, most of the nebulous impressions evoked by change of scene had gathered into substantial form. Others, however, were still in the nebulous state,—diffusing a gentle light upon Ferdinand's path. Chief among these was the mild radiance of which Miss Hofmann was the centre. For three days after his arrival Mason had been confined to his room by the aggravation of his condition consequent upon his journey. It was not till the fourth day, therefore, that he was able to renew the acquaintance so auspiciously commenced. When at last, at dinner-time, he reappeared in the drawing-room, Miss Hofmann greeted him almost as an old friend. Mason had already discovered that she was young and gracious; he now rapidly advanced to the conclusion that she was uncommonly pretty. Before dinner was over, he had made up his mind that she was neither more nor less than beautiful. Mrs. Mason had found time to give him a full account of her life. She had lost her mother in infancy, and had been adopted by her aunt in the early years of this lady's widowhood. Her father was a man of evil habits,—a drunkard, a gambler, and a rake, outlawed from decent society. His only dealings with his daughter were to write her every month or two a begging letter, she being in possession of her mother's property. Mrs. Mason had taken her niece to Europe, and given her every advantage. She had had an expensive education; she had travelled; she had gone into the world; she had been presented, like a good republican, to no less than three European sovereigns; she had been admired; she had had half a dozen offers of marriage to her aunt's knowledge, and others, perhaps, of which she was ignorant, and had refused them all. She was now twenty-six years of age, beautiful, accomplished, and *au mieux* with her bankers. She was an excellent girl, with a will of her own. "I'm very fond of her," Mrs. Mason declared, with her habitual frankness; "and I suppose she's equally fond of me; but we long ago gave up all idea of playing at mother and daughter. We have never had a disagreement since she was fifteen years old; but we have never had an agreement either. Caroline is no sentimentalist. She's honest, good-tempered, and perfectly discerning. She foresaw that we were still to spend a number of years together, and she wisely declined at the outset to affect a range of feelings that wouldn't stand the wear and tear of time. She knew that she would make a poor daughter, and she contented herself with being a good niece. A capital niece she is. In fact we're almost sisters. There are moments when I feel as if she were ten years older than I, and as if it were absurd in me to attempt to interfere with her life. I never do. She has it quite in her own hands. My attitude is little more than a state of affectionate curiosity as to what she will do with it. Of course she'll marry, sooner or later; but I'm curious to see the man of her choice. In Europe, you know, girls have no acquaintances but such as they share with their parents and guardians; and in that way I know most of the gentlemen who have tried to make themselves acceptable to my niece. There were some excellent young men in the number; but there was not one—or, rather, there was but one—for whom

Caroline cared a straw. That one she loved, I believe; but they had a quarrel, and she lost him.
She's very discreet and conciliating. I'm sure no
girl ever before got rid of half a dozen suitors with
so little offence. Ah, she's a dear, good girl!" Mrs.
Mason pursued. "She's saved me a world of trouble
in my day. And when I think what she might have
been, with her beauty, and what not! She has kept
all her suitors as friends. There are two of them
who write to her still. She doesn't answer their
letters; but once in a while she meets them, and
thanks them for writing, and that contents them.
The others are married, and Caroline remains single.
I take for granted it won't last forever. Still,
although she's *not* a sentimentalist, she'll not marry
a man she doesn't care for, merely because she's
growing old. Indeed, it's only the sentimental girls,
to my belief, that do that. They covet a man for
his money or his looks, and then give the feeling
some fine name. But there's one thing, Mr. Ferdinand," added Mrs. Mason, at the close of these
remarks, "you will be so good as not to fall in love
with my niece. I can assure you that she'll not fall
in love with you, and a hopeless passion will not
hasten your recovery. Caroline is a charming girl.
You can live with her very well without that. She's
good for common daylight, and you'll have no need
of wax-candles and ecstasies."

"Be reassured," said Ferdinand, laughing. "I'm quite too attentive to myself at present to think of any one else. Miss Hofmann might be dying for a glance of my eye, and I shouldn't hesitate to sacrifice her. It takes more than half a man to fall in love."

At the end of ten days summer had fairly set in; and Mason found it possible, and indeed profitable, to spend a large portion of his time in the open air. He was unable either to ride or to walk; and the only form of exercise which he found practicable was an occasional drive in Mrs. Mason's phaeton. On these occasions Mrs. Mason was his habitual companion. The neighborhood offered an interminable succession of beautiful drives; and poor Ferdinand took a truly exquisite pleasure in reclining idly upon a pile of cushions, warmly clad, empty-handed, silent, with only his eyes in motion, and rolling rapidly between fragrant hedges and springing crops, and beside the outskirts of woods, and along the heights which overlooked the river. Detested war was over, and all nature had ratified the peace. Mason used to gaze up into the cloudless sky until his eyes began to water, and you would have actually supposed he was shedding sentimental tears. Besides these comfortable drives with his hostess, Mason had adopted another method of inhaling the sunshine. He used frequently to spend several hours at a time on a veranda beside the house, sheltered from the observation of visitors. Here, with an arm-chair and a footstool, a cigar and half a dozen volumes of novels, to say nothing of the society of either of the ladies, and sometimes of both, he suffered the mornings to pass unmeasured and uncounted. The chief incident of these mornings was the Doctor's visit, in which, of course, there was a strong element of prose,—and very good prose, as I may add, for the Doctor was turning out an excellent fellow. But, for the rest, time unrolled itself like a gentle strain of music. Mason knew so little, from direct observation, of the *vie intime* of elegant, intelligent women, that their habits, their manners, their household motions, their principles, possessed in his view all the charm of a spectacle,—a spectacle which he contemplated with the indolence of an invalid, the sympathy of a man of taste, and a little of the awkwardness which women gladly allow, and indeed provoke, in a soldier, for the pleasure of forgiving it. It was a very simple matter to Miss Hofmann that she should be dressed in fresh crisp muslin, that her hands should be white and her attitudes felicitous; she had long since made her peace with these things. But to Mason, who was familiar only with books and men, they were objects of constant, half-dreamy contemplation. He would sit for half an hour at once, with a book on his knees and the pages unturned, scrutinizing with ingenious indirectness the simple mass of colors and contours which made up the physical personality of Miss Hofmann. There was no question as to her beauty, or as to its being a warm, sympathetic beauty, and not the cold perfection of poetry. She was the least bit taller than most women, and neither stout nor the reverse. Her hair was of a dark and lustrous brown, turning almost to black, and lending itself readily to those multitudinous ringlets which were then in fashion. Her forehead was broad, open, and serene; and her eyes of that deep and clear sea-green that you may observe of a summer's afternoon, when the declining sun shines through the rising of a wave. Her complexion was the color of perfect health. These, with her full, mild lips, her generous and flexible figure, her magnificent hands, were charms enough to occupy Mason's attention, and it was but seldom that he allowed it to be diverted. Mrs. Mason was frequently called away by her household cares, but Miss Hofmann's time was apparently quite her own. Nevertheless, it came into Ferdinand's head one day, that she gave him her company only from a sense of duty, and when, according to his wont, he had allowed this impression to ripen in his mind, he ventured to assure her that, much as he valued her society, he should be sorry to believe that her gracious bestowal of it interfered with more profitable occupations.

"I'm no companion," he said. "I don't pretend to be one. I sit here deaf and dumb, and blind and halt, patiently waiting to be healed,—waiting till this vagabond Nature of ours strolls my way, and brushes me with the hem of her garment."

"I find you very good company," Miss Hofmann replied on this occasion. "What do you take me for? The hero of a hundred fights, a young man who has been reduced to a shadow in the service of his country,—I should be very fastidious if I asked for anything better."

"O, if it's on theory!" said Mason. And, in spite of Miss Hofmann's protest, he continued to assume that it *was* on theory that he was not intolerable. But she remained true to her post, and with a sort of placid inveteracy which seemed to the young man to betray either a great deal of indifference or a great deal of self-command. "She thinks I'm stupid," he said to himself. "Of course she thinks I'm stupid. How should she think otherwise? She and her aunt have talked me over. Mrs. Mason has enumerated my virtues, and Miss Hofmann has added them up: total, a well-meaning bore. She has armed herself with patience. I must say it becomes her very well." Nothing was more natural, however, than that Mason should exaggerate the effect of his social incapacity. His remarks were desultory, but not infrequent; often trivial, but always good-humored and informal. The intervals of silence, indeed, which enlivened his conversation with Miss Hofmann, might easily have been taken for the confident pauses in the talk of old friends.

Once in a while Miss Hofmann would sit down at the piano and play to him. The veranda communicated with the little sitting-room by means of a long window, one side of which stood open. Mason would move his chair to this aperture, so that he might see the music as well as hear it. Seated at the instrument, at the farther end of the half-darkened room, with her figure in half-profile, and her features, her movements, the color of her dress, but half defined in the cool obscurity, Miss Hofmann would discourse infinite melody. Mason's eyes rested awhile on the vague white folds of her dress, on the heavy convolutions of her hair, and the gentle movement of her head in sympathy with the music. Then a single glance in the other direction revealed another picture,—the dazzling midday sky, the close-cropped lawn, lying almost black in its light, and the patient, round-backed gardener, in white shirt-sleeves, clipping the hedge or rolling the gravel. One morning, what with the music, the light, the heat, and the fragrance of the flowers,—from the perfect equilibrium of his senses, as it were,—Mason manfully went to sleep. On waking he found that he had slept an hour, and that the sun had invaded the veranda. The music had ceased; but on looking into the parlor he saw Miss Hofmann still at the piano. A gentleman was leaning on the instrument with his back toward the window, intercepting her face. Mason sat for some moments, hardly sensible, at first, of his transition to consciousness, languidly guessing at her companion's identity. In a short time his observation was quickened by the fact that the picture before him was animated by no sound of voices. The silence was unnatural, or, at the least, disagreeable. Mason moved his chair, and the gentleman looked round. The gentleman was Horace Knight. The Doctor called out, "Good morning!" from his place, and finished his conversation with Miss Hofmann before coming out to his patient. When he moved away from the piano, Mason saw the reason of his friends' silence. Miss Hofmann had been trying to decipher a difficult piece of music, the Doctor had been trying to assist her, and they had both been brought to a stop.

"What a clever fellow he is!" thought Mason. "There he stands, rattling off musical terms as if he had never thought of anything else. And yet, when he talks medicine, it's impossible to talk more to the point." Mason continued to be very well satisfied with Knight's intelligence of his case, and with his treatment of it. He had been in the country now for three weeks, and he would hesitate, indeed, to affirm that he felt materially better; but he felt more comfortable. There were moments when he feared to push the inquiry as to his real improvement, because he had a sickening apprehension that he would discover that in one or two important particulars he was worse. In the course of time he imparted these fears to his physician. "But I may be mistaken," he added, "and for this reason. During the last fortnight I have become much more sensible of my condition than while I was in town. I then accepted each additional symptom as a matter of course. The more the better, I thought. But now I expect them to give an account of themselves. Now I have a positive wish to recover."

Dr. Knight looked at his patient for a moment curiously. "You are right," he said; "a little impatience is a very good thing."

"O, I'm not impatient. I'm patient to a most ridiculous extent. I allow myself a good six months, at the very least."

"That is certainly not unreasonable," said Knight. "And will you allow me a question? Do you intend to spend those six months in this place?"

"I'm unable to answer you. I suppose I shall finish the summer here, unless the summer finishes me. Mrs. Mason will hear of nothing else. In September I hope to be well enough to go back to town, even if I'm not well enough to think of work. What do you advise?"

"I advise you to put away all thoughts of work. That is imperative.   Haven't you been at work all your life long?   Can't you spare a pitiful little twelve-month to health and idleness and pleasure?"

"Ah, pleasure, pleasure!" said Mason, ironically.

"Yes, pleasure," said the Doctor.   "What has she done to you that you should speak of her in that manner?"

"O, she bothers me," said Mason.

"You are very fastidious.   It's better to be bothered by pleasure than by pain."

"I don't deny it.   But there is a way of being indifferent to pain.   I don't mean to say that I have found it out, but in the course of my illness I have caught a glimpse of it.   But it's beyond my strength to be indifferent to pleasure.   In two words, I'm afraid of dying of kindness."

"O, nonsense!"

"Yes, it's nonsense; and yet it's not.   There would be nothing miraculous in my not getting well."

"It will be your fault if you don't.   It will prove that you're fonder of sickness than health, and that you're not fit company for sensible mortals.   Shall I tell you?" continued the Doctor, after a moment's hesitation. "When I knew you in the army, I always found you a step beyond my comprehension. You took things too hard. You had scruples and doubts about everything. And on top of it all you were devoured with the mania of appearing to take things easily and to be perfectly indifferent. You played your part very well, but you must do me the justice to confess that it *was* a part."

"I hardly know whether that's a compliment or an impertinence. I hope, at least, that you don't mean to accuse me of playing a part at the present moment."

"On the contrary. I'm your physician; you're frank."

"It's not because you're my physician that I'm frank," said Mason. "I shouldn't think of burdening you in that capacity with my miserable caprices and fancies;" and Ferdinand paused a moment. "You're a man!" he pursued, laying his hand on his companion's arm. "There's nothing here but women, Heaven reward them! I'm saturated with whispers and perfumes and smiles, and the rustling of dresses. It takes a man to understand a man."

"It takes more than a man to understand you, my dear Mason," said Knight, with a kindly smile. "But I listen."

Mason remained silent, leaning back in his chair, with his eyes wandering slowly over the wide patch of sky disclosed by the window, and his hands languidly folded on his knees. The Doctor examined him with a look half amused, half perplexed. But at last his face grew quite sober, and he contracted his brow. He placed his hand on Mason's arm and shook it gently, while Ferdinand met his gaze. The Doctor frowned, and, as he did so, his companion's mouth expanded into a placid smile. "If you don't get well," said Knight,—"if you don't get well——" and he paused.

"What will be the consequences?" asked Ferdinand, still smiling.

"I shall hate you," said Knight, half smiling, too.

Mason broke into a laugh. "What shall I care for that?"

"I shall tell people that you were a poor, spiritless fellow,—that you are no loss."

"I give you leave," said Ferdinand.

The Doctor got up. "I don't like obstinate patients," he said.

Ferdinand burst into a long, loud laugh, which ended in a fit of coughing.

"I'm getting too amusing," said Knight; "I must go."

"Nay, laugh and grow fat," cried Ferdinand. "I promise to get well." But that evening, at least, he was no better, as it turned out, for his momentary exhilaration. Before turning in for the night, he went into the drawing-room to spend half an hour with the ladies. The room was empty, but the lamp was lighted, and he sat down by the table and read a chapter in a novel. He felt excited, light-headed, light-hearted, half-intoxicated, as if he had been drinking strong coffee. He put down his book, and went over to the mantelpiece, above which hung a mirror, and looked at the reflection of his face. For almost the first time in his life he examined his features, and wondered if he were good-looking. He was able to conclude only that he looked very thin and pale, and utterly unfit for the business of life. At last he heard an opening of doors overhead, and a rustling of voluminous skirts on the stairs. Mrs. Mason came in, fresh from the hands of her maid, and dressed for a party.

"And is Miss Hofmann going?" asked Mason. He felt that his heart was beating, and that he hoped Mrs. Mason would say no. His momentary sense of strength, the mellow lamp-light, the open piano, and the absence, of the excellent woman before him, struck him as so many reasons for her remaining at home. But the sound of the young lady's descent upon the stairs was an affirmative to his question. She forthwith appeared upon the threshold, dressed in crape of a kind of violent blue, with desultory clusters of white roses. For some ten minutes Mason had the pleasure of being witness of that series of pretty movements and preparations with which women in full dress beguile the interval before their carriage is announced; their glances at the mirror, their slow assumption of their gloves, their mutual revisions and felicitations.

"Isn't she lovely?" said Miss Hofmann to the young man, nodding at her aunt, who looked every inch the handsome woman that she was.

"Lovely, lovely, lovely!" said Ferdinand, so emphatically, that Miss Hofmann transferred her glance to him; while Mrs. Mason good-humoredly turned her back, and Caroline saw that Mason was engaged in a survey of her own person.

Miss Hofmann smiled discreetly. "I wish very much you might come," she said.

"I shall go to bed," answered Ferdinand, simply.

"Well, that's much better. We shall go to bed at two o'clock. Meanwhile I shall caper about the rooms to the sound of a piano and fiddle, and Aunt Maria will sit against the wall with her toes tucked under a chair. Such is life!"

"You'll dance then," said Mason.

"I shall dance. Dr. Knight has invited me."

"Does he dance well, Caroline?" asked Mrs. Mason.

"That remains to be seen. I have a strong impression that he does not."

"Why?" asked Ferdinand.

"He does so many other things well."

"That's no reason," said Mrs. Mason. "Do you dance, Ferdinand?"

Ferdinand shook his head.

"I like a man to dance," said Caroline, "and yet I like him not to dance."

"That's a very womanish speech, my dear," said Mrs. Mason.

"I suppose it is. It's inspired by my white gloves and my low dress, and my roses. When once a woman gets on such things, Colonel Mason, expect nothing but nonsense.—Aunt Maria," the young lady continued, "will you button my glove?"

"Let me do it," said Ferdinand. "Your aunt has her gloves on."

"Thank you." And Miss Hofmann extended a long, white arm, and drew back with her other hand the bracelet from her wrist. Her glove had three buttons, and Mason performed the operation with great deliberation and neatness.

"And now," said he, gravely, "I hear the carriage. You want me to put on your shawl."

"If you please,"—Miss Hofmann passed her full white drapery into his hands, and then turned about her fair shoulders. Mason solemnly covered them, while the waiting-maid, who had come in, performed the same service for the elder lady.

"Good by," said the latter, giving him her hand.

"You're not to come out into the air." And Mrs. Mason, attended by her maid, transferred herself to the carriage. Miss Hofmann gathered up her loveliness, and prepared to follow. Ferdinand stood leaning against the parlor door, watching her; and as she rustled past him she nodded farewell with a silent smile. A characteristic smile, Mason thought it,—a smile in which there was no expectation of triumph and no affectation of reluctance, but just the faintest suggestion of perfectly good-humored resignation. Mason went to the window and saw the carriage roll away with its lighted lamps, and then stood looking out into the darkness. The sky was cloudy. As he turned away the maid-servant came in, and took from the table a pair of rejected gloves. "I hope you're feeling better, sir," she said, politely.

"Thank you, I think I am."

"It's a pity you couldn't have gone with the ladies."

"I'm not well enough yet to think of such things," said Mason, trying to smile. But as he walked across the floor he felt himself attacked by a sudden sensation, which cannot be better described than as a general collapse. He felt dizzy, faint, and sick. His head swam and his knees trembled. "I'm ill," he said, sitting down on the sofa; "you must call William."

William speedily arrived, and conducted the young man to his room. "What on earth had you been doing, sir?" asked this most irreproachable of serving-men, as he helped him to undress.

Ferdinand was silent a moment. "I had been putting on Miss Hofmann's shawl," he said.

"Is that all, sir?"

"And I had been buttoning her glove."

"Well, sir, you must be very prudent."

"So it appears," said Ferdinand.

He slept soundly, however, and the next morning was the better for it. "I'm certainly better," he said to himself, as he slowly proceeded to his toilet. "A month ago such an attack as that of last evening would have effectually banished sleep. Courage, then. The Devil isn't dead, but he's dying."

In the afternoon he received a visit from Horace Knight. "So you danced last evening at Mrs. Bradshaw's," he said to his friend.

"Yes, I danced. It's a great piece of frivolity for a man in my position; but I thought there would be no harm in doing it just once, to show them I know how. My abstinence in future will tell the better. Your ladies were there. I danced with Miss Hofmann. She was dressed in blue, and she was the most beautiful woman in the room. Every one was talking about it."

"I saw her," said Mason, "before she went off."

"You should have seen her there," said Knight. "The music, the excitement, the spectators, and all that, bring out a woman's beauty."

"So I suppose," said Ferdinand.

"What strikes me," pursued the Doctor, "is her —what shall I call it?—her vitality, her quiet buoyancy. Of course, you didn't see her when she came home? If you had, you would have noticed, unless I'm very much mistaken, that she was as fresh and elastic at two o'clock as she had been at ten. While all the other women looked tired and jaded and used up, she alone showed no signs of exhaustion. She was neither pale nor flushed, but still light-footed, rosy, and erect. She's solid. You see I can't help looking at such things as a physician. She has a magnificent organization. Among all those other poor girls she seemed to have something of the inviolable strength of a goddess;" and Knight smiled frankly as he entered the region of eloquence. "She wears her artificial roses and dew-drops as if she had gathered them on the mountain-tops, instead of buying them in Broadway. She moves with long steps, her dress rustles, and to a man of fancy it's the sound of Diana on the forest-leaves."

Ferdinand nodded assent. "So you're a man of fancy," he said.

"Of course I am," said the Doctor.

Ferdinand was not inclined to question his

friend's estimate of Miss Hofmann, nor to weigh his words. They only served to confirm an impression which was already strong in his own mind. Day by day he had felt the growth of this impression. "He must be a strong man who would approach her," he said to himself. "He must be as vigorous and elastic as she herself, or in the progress of courtship she will leave him far behind. He must be able to forget his lungs and his liver and his digestion. To have broken down in his country's defence, even, will avail him nothing. What is that to her? She needs a man who has defended his country without breaking down,—a being complete, intact, well seasoned, invulnerable. Then,—then," thought Ferdinand, "perhaps she will consider him. Perhaps it will be to refuse him. Perhaps, like Diana, to whom Knight compares her, she is meant to live alone. It's certain, at least, that she is able to wait. She will be young at forty-five. Women who are young at forty-five are perhaps not the most interesting women. They are likely to have felt for nobody and for nothing. But it's often less their own fault than that of the men and women about them. This one at least *can* feel; the thing is to move her. Her soul is an instrument of a hundred strings, only it takes a strong hand to draw sound. Once really touched, they will reverberate for ever and ever."

In fine, Mason was in love. It will be seen that his passion was not arrogant nor uncompromising; but, on the contrary, patient, discreet, and modest, —almost timid. For ten long days, the most memorable days of his life,—days which, if he had kept a journal, would have been left blank,—he held his tongue. He would have suffered anything rather than reveal his emotions, or allow them to come accidentally to Miss Hofmann's knowledge. He would cherish them in silence until he should feel in all his sinews that he was himself again, and then he would open his heart. Meanwhile he would be patient; he would be the most irreproachable, the most austere, the most insignificant of convalescents. He was as yet unfit to touch her, to look at her, to speak to her. A man was not to go a wooing in his dressing-gown and slippers.

There came a day, however, when, in spite of his high resolves, Ferdinand came near losing his balance. Mrs. Mason had arranged with him to drive in the phaeton after dinner. But it befell that, an hour before the appointed time, she was sent for by by a neighbor who had been taken ill.

"But it's out of the question that you should lose your drive," said Miss Hofmann, who brought him her aunt's apologies. "If you are still disposed to go, I shall be happy to take the reins. I shall not be as good company as Aunt Maria, but perhaps I shall be as good company as Thomas." It was settled, accordingly, that Miss Hofmann should act as her aunt's substitute, and at five o'clock the phaeton left the door. The first half of their drive was passed in silence; and almost the first words they exchanged were as they finally drew near to a space of enclosed ground, beyond which, through the trees at its farther extremity, they caught a glimpse of a turn in the river. Miss Hofmann involuntarily pulled up. The sun had sunk low, and the cloudless western sky glowed with rosy yellow. The trees which concealed the view flung over the grass a great screen of shadow, which reached out into the road. Between their scattered stems gleamed the broad, white current of the Hudson. Our friends both knew the spot. Mason had seen it from a boat, when one morning a gentleman in the neighborhood, thinking to do him a kindness, had invited him to take a short sail; and with Miss Hofmann it had long been a frequent resort.

"How beautiful!" she said, as the phaeton stopped.

"Yes, if it wasn't for those trees," said Ferdinand. "They conceal the best part of the view."

"I should rather say they indicate it," answered his companion. "From here they conceal it; but they suggest to you to make your way in, and lose yourself behind them, and enjoy the prospect in privacy."

"But you can't take a vehicle in."

"No: there is only a footpath, although I have ridden in. One of these days, when you're stronger, you must drive to this point, and get out, and walk over to the bank."

Mason was silent a moment,—a moment during which he felt in his limbs the tremor of a bold resolution. "I noticed the place the day I went out on the water with Mr. McCarthy. I immediately marked it as my own. The bank is quite high, and the trees make a little amphitheatre on its summit. I think there's a bench."

"Yes, there are two benches," said Caroline.

"Suppose, then, we try it now," said Mason, with an effort.

"But you can never walk over that meadow. You see it's broken ground. And, at all events, I can't consent to your going alone."

"That, madam," said Ferdinand, rising to his feet in the phaeton, "is a piece of folly I should never think of proposing. Yonder is a house, and in it there are people. Can't we drive thither, and place the horse in their custody?"

"Nothing is more easy, if you insist upon it. The house is occupied by a German family with a couple of children, who are old friends of mine. When I come here on horseback they always clamor for 'coppers.' From their little garden the walk is shorter."

So Miss Hofmann turned the horse toward the cottage, which stood at the head of a lane, a few yards from the road. A little boy and girl, with bare heads and bare feet,—the former members very white and the latter very black,—came out to meet her. Caroline greeted them good-humoredly in German. The girl, who was the elder, consented to watch the horse, while the boy volunteered to show the visitors the shortest way to the river. Mason reached the point in question without great fatigue, and found a prospect which would have repaid even greater trouble. To the right and to the left, a hundred feet below them, stretched the broad channel of the seaward-shifting waters. In the distance rose the gentle masses of the Catskills with all the intervening region vague and neutral in the gathering twilight. A faint odor of coolness came up to their faces from the stream below.

"You can sit down," said the little boy, doing the honors.

"Yes, Colonel, sit down," said Caroline. "You've already been on your feet too much."

Ferdinand obediently seated himself, unable to deny that he was glad to do so. Miss Hofmann released from her grasp the skirts which she had gathered up in her passage from the phaeton, and strolled to the edge of the cliff, where she stood for some moments talking with her little guide. Mason could only hear that she was speaking German. After the lapse of a few moments Miss Hofmann turned back, still talking—or rather listening—to the child.

"He's very pretty," she said in French, as she stopped before Ferdinand.

Mason broke into a laugh. "To think," said he, "that that little youngster should forbid us the use of two languages! Do you speak French, my child?"

"No," said the boy, sturdily, "I speak German."

"Ah, there I can't follow you!"

The child stared a moment, and then replied, with pardonable irrelevancy, "I'll show you the way down to the water."

"There I can't follow you either. I hope *you'll* not go, Miss Hofmann," added the young man, observing a movement on Caroline's part.

"Is it hard?" she asked of the child.

"No, it's easy."

"Will I tear my dress?"

The child shook his head; and Caroline descended the bank under his guidance.

As some moments elapsed before she reappeared, Ferdinand ventured to the edge of the cliff, and looked down. She was sitting on a rock on the narrow margin of sand, with her hat in her lap, twisting the feather in her fingers. In a few moments it seemed to Ferdinand that he caught the tones of her voice, wafted upward as if she were gently singing. He listened intently, and at last succeeded in distinguishing several words; they were German. "Confound her German!" thought the young man. Suddenly Miss Hofmann rose from her seat, and, after a short interval, reappeared on the platform. "What did you find down there?" asked Ferdinand, almost savagely.

"Nothing,—a little strip of a beach and a pile of stones."

"You *have* torn your dress," said Mason.

Miss Hofmann surveyed her drapery. "Where, if you please?"

"There, in front." And Mason extended his walking-stick, and inserted it into the injured fold of muslin. There was a certain graceless *brusquerie* in the movement which attracted Miss Hofmann's attention. She looked at her companion, and, seeing that his face was discomposed, fancied that he was annoyed at having been compelled to wait.

"Thank you," she said; "it's easily mended. And now suppose we go back."

"No, not yet," said Ferdinand. "We have plenty of time."

"Plenty of time to catch cold," said Miss Hofmann, kindly.

Mason had planted his stick where he had let it fall on withdrawing it from contact with his companion's skirts, and stood leaning against it, with his eyes on the young girl's face. "What if I do catch cold?" he asked abruptly.

"Come, don't talk nonsense," said Miss Hofmann.

"I never was more serious in my life." And, pausing a moment, he drew a couple of steps nearer. She had gathered her shawl closely about her, and stood with her arms lost in it, holding her elbows. "I don't mean that quite literally," Mason continued. "I wish to get well, on the whole. But there are moments when this perpetual self-coddling seems beneath the dignity of man, and I'm tempted to purchase one short hour of enjoyment, of happiness, at the cost—well, at the cost of my life if necessary!"

This was a franker speech than Ferdinand had yet made; the reader may estimate his habitual reserve. Miss Hofmann must have been somewhat surprised, and even slightly puzzled. But it was plain that he expected a rejoinder.

"I don't know what temptation you may have had," she answered, smiling; "but I confess that I can think of none in your present circumstances likely to involve the great sacrifice you speak of. What you say, Colonel Mason, is half——"

"Half what?"

"Half ungrateful. Aunt Maria flatters herself that she has made existence as easy and as peaceful for you—as stupid, if you like—as it can possibly be for a—a clever man. And now, after all, to accuse her of introducing temptations."

"Your aunt Maria is the best of women, Miss Hofmann," said Mason. "But I'm not a clever man. I'm deplorably weak-minded. Very little things excite me. Very small pleasures are gigantic temptations. I would give a great deal, for instance, to stay here with you for half an hour."

It is a delicate question whether Miss Hofmann now ceased to be perplexed; whether she discerned in the young man's accents—it was his tone, his attitude, his eyes that were fully significant, rather than his words—an intimation of that sublime and simple truth in the presence of which a wise woman puts off coquetry and prudery, and stands invested with perfect charity. But charity is nothing if not discreet; and Miss Hofmann may very well have effected the little transaction I speak of, and yet have remained, as she did remain, gracefully wrapped in her shawl, with the same serious smile on her face. Ferdinand's heart was thumping under his waistcoat; the words in which he might tell her

that he loved her were fluttering there like frightened birds in a storm-shaken cage. Whether his
lips would form them or not depended on the next
words she uttered. On the faintest sign of defiance
or of impatience he would really give her something
to coquet withal. I repeat that I do not undertake
to follow Miss Hofmann's feelings; I only know
that her words were those of a woman of great in-
stincts. "My dear Colonel Mason," she said, "I
wish we might remain here the whole evening. The
moments are quite too pleasant to be wantonly sac-
rificed. I simply put you on your conscience. If
you believe that you can safely do so,—that you'll
not have some dreadful chill in consequence,—let
us by all means stay awhile. If you do not so believe, let us go back to the carriage. There is no
good reason, that I see, for our behaving like children."

If Miss Hofmann apprehended a scene,—I do not
assert that she did,—she was saved. Mason ex-
tracted from her words a delicate assurance that
he could afford to wait. "You're an angel, Miss
Hofmann," he said, as a sign that this kindly assurance had been taken. "I think we had better go
back."

Miss Hofmann accordingly led the way along
the path, and Ferdinand slowly followed. A man
who has submitted to a woman's wisdom generally

feels bound to persuade himself that he has surrendered at discretion. I suppose it was in this spirit that Mason said to himself as he walked along, "Well, I got what I wanted."

The next morning he was again an invalid. He woke up with symptoms which as yet he had scarcely felt at all; and he was obliged to acknowledge the bitter truth that, small as it was, his adventure had exceeded his strength. The walk, the evening air, the dampness of the spot, had combined to produce a violent attack of fever. As soon as it became plain that, in vulgar terms, he was "in for it," he took his heart in his hands and succumbed. As his condition grew worse, he was fortunately relieved from the custody of this valuable organ, with all it contained of hopes delayed and broken projects, by several intervals of prolonged unconsciousness.

For three weeks he was a very sick man. For a couple of days his recovery was doubted of. Mrs. Mason attended him with inexhaustible patience and with the solicitude of real affection. She was resolved that greedy Death should not possess himself, through any fault of hers, of a career so full of bright possibilities and of that active gratitude which a good-natured elderly woman would relish, as she felt that of her *protégé* to be. Her vigils were finally rewarded. One fine morning poor, long-silent Ferdinand found words to tell her that

he was better. His recovery was very slow, however, and it ceased several degrees below the level
from which he had originally fallen. He was thus
twice a convalescent,—a sufficiently miserable fellow. He professed to be very much surprised to
find himself still among the living. He remained
silent and grave, with a newly contracted fold in
his forehead, like a man honestly perplexed at the
vagaries of destiny. "It must be," he said to Mrs.
Mason,—"it must be that I am reserved for great
things."

In order to insure absolute quiet in the house,
Ferdinand learned Miss Hofmann had removed herself to the house of a friend, at a distance of some
five miles. On the first day that the young man was
well enough to sit in his arm-chair Mrs. Mason
spoke of her niece's return, which was fixed for the
morrow. "She will want very much to see you,"
she said. "When she comes, may I bring her into
your room?"

"Good heavens, no!" said Ferdinand, to whom
the idea was very disagreeable. He met her accordingly at dinner, three days later. He left his
room at the dinner hour, in company with Dr.
Knight, who was taking his departure. In the hall
they encountered Mrs. Mason, who invited the Doctor to remain, in honor of his patient's reappearance
in society. The Doctor hesitated a moment, and,

as he did so, Ferdinand heard Miss Hofmann's step
descending the stair. He turned towards her just
in time to catch on her face the vanishing of a
glance of intelligence. As Mrs. Mason's back was
against the staircase, her glance was evidently meant
for Knight. He excused himself on the plea of an
engagement, to Mason's regret, while ;the latter
greeted the younger lady. Mrs. Mason proposed
another day,—the following Sunday; the Doctor
assented, and it was not till some time later that
Ferdinand found himself wondering why Miss Hofmann should have forbidden him to remain. He
rapidly perceived that during the period of their
separation this young lady had lost none of her
charms; on the contrary, they were more irresistible
than ever. It seemed to Mason, moreover, that they
were bound together by a certain pensive gentle-
ness, a tender, submissive look, which he had hitherto failed to observe. Mrs. Mason's own remarks
assured him that he was not the victim of an illusion.

"I wonder what is the matter with Caroline,"
she said. "If it were not that she tells me that she
never was better, I should believe she is feeling un-
well. I've never seen her so simple and gentle. She
looks like a person who has a great fright,—a fright
not altogether unpleasant."

"She has been staying in a house full of people,"

said Mason. "She has been excited, and amused, and preoccupied; she returns to you and me (excuse the juxtaposition,—it exists)—a kind of reaction asserts itself." Ferdinand's explanation was ingenious rather than plausible.

Mrs. Mason had a better one. "I have an impression," she said, "George Stapleton, the second of the sons, is an old admirer of Caroline's. It's hard to believe that he could have been in the house with her for a fortnight without renewing his suit, in some form or other."

Ferdinand was not made uneasy, for he had seen and talked with Mr. George Stapleton,—a young man, very good-looking, very good-natured, very clever, very rich, and very unworthy, as he conceived, of Miss Hofmann. "You don't mean to say that your niece has listened to him," he answered, calmly enough.

"Listened, yes. He has made himself agreeable, and he has succeeded in making an impression,—a temporary impression," added Mrs. Mason with a business-like air.

"I can't believe it," said Ferdinand.

"Why not? He's a very nice fellow."

"Yes,—yes," said Mason, "very nice, indeed. He's very rich, too." And here the talk was interrupted by Caroline's entrance.

On Sunday the two ladies went to church. It

was not till after they had gone that Ferdinand left
his room. He came into the little parlor, took up
a book, and felt something of the stir of his old intellectual life. Would he ever again know what it
was to work? In the course of an hour the ladies
came in, radiant with devotional millinery. Mrs.
Mason soon went out again, leaving the others together. Miss Hofmann asked Ferdinand what he
had been reading; and he was thus led to declare
that he really believed he should, after all, get the
use of his head again. She listened with all the respect which an intelligent woman who leads an idle
life necessarily feels for a clever man when he con-
sents to make her in some degree the confidant of
his intellectual purposes. Quickened by her delicious
sympathy, her grave attention, and her intelligent
questions, he was led to unbosom himself of several
of his dearest convictions and projects. It was easy
that from this point the conversation should advance to matters of belief and hope in general. Before he knew it, it had done so; and he had thus
the great satisfaction of discussing with the woman
on whom of all others his selfish and personal happiness was most dependent those great themes in
whose expansive magnitude persons and pleasures
and passions are absorbed and extinguished, and in
whose austere effulgence the brightest divinities of
earth remit their shining. Serious passions are a

good preparation for the highest kinds of speculation. Although Ferdinand was urging no suit whatever upon his companion, and consciously, at least, making use in no degree of the emotion which accompanied her presence, it is certain that, as they formed themselves, his conceptions were the clearer for being the conceptions of a man in love. And, as for Miss Hofmann, her attention could not, to all appearances, have been more lively, nor her perception more delicate, if the atmosphere of her own intellect had been purified by the sacred fires of a responsive passion.

Knight duly made his appearance at dinner, and proved himself once more the entertaining gentleman whom our friends had long since learned to appreciate. But Mason, fresh from his contest with morals and metaphysics, was forcibly struck with the fact that he was one of those men from whom these sturdy beggars receive more kicks than halfpence. He was nevertheless obliged to admit, that, if he was not a man of principles, he was thoroughly a man of honor. After dinner the company adjourned to the piazza, where, in the course of half an hour, the Doctor proposed to Miss Hofmann to take a turn in the grounds. All around the lawn there wound a narrow footpath, concealed from view in spots by clusters of shrubbery. Ferdinand and his hostess sat watching their retreating figures as

they slowly measured the sinuous strip of gravel;
Miss Hofmann's light dress and the Doctor's white
waistcoat gleaming at intervals through the dark
verdure. At the end of twenty minutes they returned to the house. The doctor came back only
to make his bow and to take his departure; and,
when he had gone, Miss Hofmann retired to her
own room. The next morning she mounted her
horse, and rode over to see the friend with whom
she had stayed during Mason's fever. Ferdinand
saw her pass his window, erect in the saddle, with
her horse scattering the gravel with his nervous
steps. Shortly afterwards Mrs. Mason came into
the room, sat down by the young man, made her
habitual inquiries as to his condition, and then
paused in such a way as that he instantly felt that
she had something to tell him. "You've something
to tell me," he said; "what is it?"

Mrs. Mason blushed a little, and laughed. "I
was first made to promise to keep it a secret," she
said. "If I'm so transparent now that I have leave
to tell it, what should I be if I hadn't? Guess."

Ferdinand shook his head peremptorily. "I give
it up."

"Caroline is engaged."

"To whom?"

"Not to Mr. Stapleton,—to Dr. Knight."

Ferdinand was silent a moment; but he neither

changed color nor dropped his eyes. Then, at last, "Did she wish you not to tell me?" he asked.

"She wished me to tell no one. But I prevailed upon her to let me tell *you*."

"Thank you," said Ferdinand with a little bow— and an immense irony.

"It's a great surprise," continued Mrs. Mason. "I never suspected it. And there I was talking about Mr. Stapleton! I don't see how they have managed it. Well, I suppose it's for the best. But it seems odd that Caroline should have refused so many superior offers, to put up at last with Dr. Knight."

Ferdinand had felt for an instant as if the power of speech was deserting him; but volition nailed it down with a great muffled hammer-blow.

"She might do worse," he said mechanically.

Mrs. Mason glanced at him as if struck by the sound of his voice. "You're not surprised, then?"

"I hardly know. I never fancied there was anything between them, and yet, now that I look back, there has been nothing against it. They have talked of each other neither too much nor too little. Upon my soul, they're an accomplished couple!" Glancing back at his friend's constant reserve and self-possession, Ferdinand—strange as it may seem— could not repress a certain impulse of sympathetic admiration. He had had no vulgar rival. "Yes," he repeated gravely, "she might do worse."

"I suppose she might. He's poor, but he's clever; and I'm sure I hope to Heaven he loves her!"

Ferdinand said nothing.

"May I ask," he resumed at length, "whether they became engaged yesterday, on that walk around the lawn?"

"No; it would be fine if they had, under our very noses! It was all done while Caroline was at the Stapletons'. It was agreed between them yesterday that she should tell me at once."

"And when are they to be married?"

"In September, if possible. Caroline told me to tell you that she counts upon your staying for the wedding."

"Staying where?" asked Mason, with a little nervous laugh.

"Staying here, of course,—in the house."

Ferdinand looked his hostess full in the eyes, taking her hand as he did so. " 'The funeral baked meats did coldly furnish forth the marriage tables.' "

"Ah, hold your tongue!" cried Mrs. Mason, pressing his hand. "How can you be so horrible? When Caroline leaves me, Ferdinand, I shall be quite alone. The tie which binds us together will be very much slackened by her marriage. I can't help thinking that it was never very close, when I con-

sider that I've had no part in the most important
step of her life. I don't complain. I suppose it's
natural enough. Perhaps it's the fashion,—come in
with striped petticoats and pea-jackets. Only it
makes me feel like an old woman. It removes me
twenty years at a bound from my own engagement,
and the day I burst out crying on my mother's neck
because your uncle had told a young girl I knew,
that he thought I had beautiful eyes. Now-a-days
I suppose they tell the young ladies themselves, and
have them cry on their own necks. It's a great saving of time. But I shall miss Caroline all the same;
and then, Ferdinand, I shall make a great deal of
you."

"The more the better," said Ferdinand, with the
same laugh; and at this moment Mrs. Mason was
called away.

Ferdinand had not been a soldier for nothing.
He had received a heavy blow, and he resolved to
bear it like a man. He refused to allow himself a
single moment of self-compassion. On the contrary, he spared himself none of the hard names offered by his passionate vocabulary. For not guessing Caroline's secret, he was perhaps excusable.
Women were all inscrutable, and this one especially
so. But Knight was a man like himself,—a man
whom he esteemed, but whom he was loath to credit
with a deeper and more noiseless current of feeling

than his own, for his own was no babbling brook, betraying its course through green leaves. Knight had loved modestly and decently, but frankly and heartily, like a man who was not ashamed of what he was doing, and if he had not found it out it was his own fault. What else had he to do? He had been a besotted day-dreamer, while his friend had simply been a genuine lover. He deserved his injury, and he would bear it in silence. He had been unable to get well on an illusion; he would now try getting well on a truth. This was stern treatment, the reader will admit, likely to kill if it didn't cure.

Miss Hofmann was absent for several hours. At dinner-time she had not returned, and Mrs. Mason and the young man accordingly sat down without her. After dinner Ferdinand went into the little parlor, quite indifferent as to how soon he met her. Seeing or not seeing her, time hung equally heavy. Shortly after her companions had risen from table, she rode up to the door, dismounted, tired and hungry, passed directly into the dining-room, and sat down to eat in her habit. In half an hour she came out, and, crossing the hall on her way upstairs, saw Mason in the parlor. She turned round, and, gathering up her long skirts with one hand, while she held a little sweet-cake to her lips with the other, stopped at the door to bid him good day. He left his chair, and went towards her. Her face wore a somewhat weary smile.

"So you're going to be married," he began abruptly.

Miss Hofmann assented with a slight movement of her head.

"I congratulate you. Excuse me if I don't do it with the best grace. I feel all I dare to feel."

"Don't be afraid," said Caroline, smiling, and taking a bite from her cake.

"I'm not sure that it's not more unexpected than even such things have a right to be. There's no doubt about it."

"None whatever."

"Well, Knight's a very good fellow. I haven't seen him yet," he pursued, as Caroline was silent. "I don't know that I'm in any hurry to see him. But I mean to talk to him. I mean to tell him that if he doesn't do his duty by you, I shall——"

"Well?"

"I shall remind him of it."

"O, I shall do that," said Miss Hofmann.

Ferdinand looked at her gravely. "By Heaven! you know," he cried with intensity, "it must be either one thing or the other."

"I don't understand you."

"O, I understand myself. You're not a woman to be thrown away, Miss Hofmann."

Caroline made a gesture of impatience. "I don't understand you," she repeated. "You must excuse me. I'm very tired." And she went rapidly up-stairs.

On the following day Ferdinand had an opportunity to make his compliments to the Doctor. "I don't congratulate you on doing it," he said, "so much as on the way you've done it."

"What do you know about the way?" asked Knight.

"Nothing whatever. That's just it. You took good care of that. And you're to be married in the autumn?"

"I hope so. Very quietly, I suppose. The Parson to do it, and Mrs. Mason and my mother and you to see it's done properly." And the Doctor put his hand on Ferdinand's shoulder.

"O, I'm the last person to choose," said Mason. "If he were to omit anything, I should take good care not to cry out." It is often said, that, next to great joy, no state of mind is so frolicsome as great distress. It was in virtue of this truth, I suppose, that Ferdinand was able to be facetious. He kept his spirits. He talked and smiled and lounged about with the same deferential languor as before. During the interval before the time appointed for the wedding it was agreed between the parties interested that Miss Hofmann should go over and spend a few days with her future mother-in-law, where she might partake more freely and privately than at home of the pleasure of her lover's company. She was absent a week; a week during which Ferdinand was thrown entirely upon his hostess for entertainment and diversion,—things he had a very keen sense of needing. There were moments when it seemed to him that he was living by mere force of will, and that, if he loosened the screws for a single instant, he would sink back upon his bed again, and never leave it. He had forbidden himself to think of Caroline, and had prescribed a course of meditation upon that other mistress, his first love, with whom he had long since exchanged pledges,—she of a hundred names,—work, letters, philosophy, fame. But, after Caroline had gone, it was supremely difficult not to think of her. Even in absence she was supremely conspicuous. The most that Ferdinand could do was to take refuge in books,—an immense number of which he now read, fiercely, passionately, voraciously,—in conversation with Mrs. Mason, and in such society as he found in his path. Mrs. Mason was a great gossip, —a gossip on a scale so magnificent as to transform the foible into a virtue. A gossip, moreover, of imagination, dealing with the future as well as the present and the past,—with a host of delightful half-possibilities, as well as with stale hyper-verities.

With her, then, Ferdinand talked of his own future, into which she entered with the most outspoken and intelligent sympathy. "A man," he declared, "couldn't do better; and a man certainly would do worse." Mrs. Mason arranged a European tour and residence for her nephew, in the manner of one who knew her ground. Caroline once married, she herself would go abroad, and fix herself in one of the several capitals in which an American widow with an easy income may contrive to support existence. She would make her dwelling a base of supplies— a *pied à terre*—for Ferdinand, who should take his time to it, and visit every accessible spot in Europe and the East. She would leave him free to go and come as he pleased, and to live as he listed; and I may say that, thanks to Mrs. Mason's observation of Continental manners, this broad allowance covered in her view quite as much as it did in poor Ferdinand's, who had never been out of his own country. All that she would ask of him would be to show himself say twice a year in her drawing-room, and to tell her stories of what he had seen; that drawing-room which she already saw in her mind's eye,—a compact little *entresol* with tapestry hangings in the doorways and a coach-house in the court attached. Mrs. Mason was not a severe moralist; but she was quite too sensible a woman to wish to demoralize her nephew, and to persuade him to

trifle with his future,—that future of which the war
had already made light, in its own grim fashion.
Nay, she loved him; she thought him the cleverest,
the most promising, of young men. She looked to
the day when his name would be on men's lips, and
it would be a great piece of good fortune to have
very innocently married his uncle. Herself a great
observer of men and manners, she wished to give
him advantages which had been sterile in her own
case.

In the way of society, Ferdinand made calls with
his hostess, went out twice to dine, and caused Mrs.
Mason herself to entertain company at dinner. He
presided on these occasions with distinguished good
grace. It happened, moreover, that invitations had
been out some days for a party at the Stapletons',
—Miss Hofmann's friends,—and that, as there was
to be no dancing, Ferdinand boldly announced his
intention of going thither. "Who knows?" he said;
"it may do me more good than harm. We can go
late, and come away early." Mrs. Mason doubted
of the wisdom of the act; but she finally assented,
and prepared herself. It was late when they left
home, and when they arrived the rooms—rooms of
exceptional vastness—were at their fullest. Mason
received on this his first appearance in society a most
flattering welcome, and in a very few moments
found himself in exclusive possession of Miss Edith

Stapleton, Caroline's particular friend. This young
lady has had no part in our story, because our story
is perforce short, and condemned to pick and choose
its constituent elements. With the least bit wider
compass we might long since have whispered to the
reader, that Miss Stapleton—who was a charming
girl—had conceived a decided preference for our
Ferdinand over all other men whomsoever. That
Ferdinand was utterly ignorant of the circumstance
is our excuse for passing it by; and we linger upon
it, therefore, only long enough to suggest that the
young girl must have been very happy at this particular moment.

"Is Miss Hofmann here?" Mason asked as he
accompanied her into an adjoining room.

"Do you call that being here?" said Miss Stapleton, looking across the apartment. Mason, too,
looked across.

There he beheld Miss Hofmann, full-robed in
white, standing fronted by a semicircle of no less
than five gentlemen,—all good-looking and splendid. Her head and shoulders rose serene from the
bouillonnement of her beautiful dress, and she
looked and listened with that half-abstracted air
which is pardonable in a woman beset by half a
dozen admirers. When Caroline's eyes fell upon
her friend, she stared a moment, surprised, and
then made him the most gracious bow in the world,

—a bow so gracious that her little circle half divided itself to let it pass, and looked around to see where the deuce it was going. Taking advantage of this circumstance, Miss Hofmann advanced several steps. Ferdinand went towards her, and there, in sight of a hundred men and as many women, she gave him her hand, and smiled upon him with extraordinary sweetness. They went back together to Miss Stapleton, and Caroline made him sit down, she and her friend placing themselves on either side. For half an hour Ferdinand had the honor of engrossing the attention of the two most charming girls present,—and, thanks to this distinction, indeed the attention of the whole company. After which the two young ladies had him introduced successively to every maiden and matron in the assembly in the least remarkable for loveliness or wit. Ferdinand rose to the level of the occasion, and conducted himself with unprecedented gallantry. Upon others he made, of course, the best impression, but to himself he was an object almost of awe. I am compelled to add, however, that he was obliged to fortify himself with repeated draughts of wine; and that even with the aid of this artificial stimulant he was unable to conceal from Mrs. Mason and his physician that he was looking far too much like an invalid to be properly where he was.

"Was there ever anything like the avidity of

these dreadful girls?" said Mrs. Mason to the Doctor. "They'll let a man swoon at their feet sooner than abridge a *tête-à-tête* that amuses them. Then they'll have up another. Look at little Miss Mc-Carthy, yonder, with Ferdinand and George Stapleton before her. She's got them contradicting each other, and she looks like a Roman fast lady at the circus. What does she care so long as she makes her evening? They like a man to look as if he were going to die,—it's interesting."

Knight went over to his friend, and told him sternly that it was high time he should be at home and in bed. "You're looking horribly," he added shrewdly, as Ferdinand resisted.

"You're *not* looking horribly, Colonel Mason," said Miss McCarthy, a very audacious little person, overhearing this speech.

"It isn't a matter of taste, madam," said the Doctor, angrily; "it's a fact." And he led away his patient.

Ferdinand insisted that he had not hurt himself, that, on the contrary, he was feeling uncommonly well; but his face contradicted him. He continued for two or three days more to play at "feeling well," with a courage worthy of a better cause. Then at last he let disease have its way. He settled himself on his pillows, and fingered his watch, and began to wonder how many revolutions he would still witness of those exquisite little needles. The Doctor came, and gave him a sound rating for what he called his imprudence. Ferdinand heard him out patiently; and then assured him that prudence or imprudence had nothing to do with it; that death had taken fast hold of him, and that now his only concern was to make easy terms with his captor. In the course of the same day he sent for a lawyer and altered his will. He had no known relatives, and his modest patrimony stood bequeathed to a gentleman of his acquaintance who had no real need of it. He now divided it into two unequal portions, the smaller of which he devised to William Bowles, Mrs. Mason's man-servant and his personal attendant; and the larger—which represented a considerable sum—to Horace Knight. He informed Mrs. Mason of these arrangements, and was pleased to have her approval.

From this moment his strength began rapidly to ebb, and the shattered fragments of his long-resisting will floated down its shallow current into dissolution. It was useless to attempt to talk, to beguile the interval, to watch the signs, or to count the hours. A constant attendant was established at his side, and Mrs. Mason appeared only at infrequent moments. The poor woman felt that her heart was broken, and spent a great deal of time in weeping. Miss Hofmann remained, naturally, at

Mrs. Knight's. "As far as I can judge," Horace had said, "it will be a matter of a week. But it's the most extraordinary case I ever heard of. The man was steadily getting well." On the fifth day he had driven Miss Hofmann home, at her suggestion that it was no more than decent that she should give the young man some little sign of sympathy. Horace went up to Ferdinand's bedside, and found the poor fellow in the languid middle condition between sleeping and waking in which he had passed the last forty-eight hours. "Colonel," he asked gently, "do you think you could see Caroline?"

For all answer, Ferdinand opened his eyes. Horace went out, and led his companion back into the darkened room. She came softly up to the bedside, stood looking down for a moment at the sick man, and then stooped over him.

"I thought I'd come and make you a little visit," she said. "Does it disturb you?"

"Not in the least," said Mason, looking her steadily in the eyes. "Not half as much as it would have done a week ago. Sit down."

"Thank you. Horace won't let me. I'll come again."

"You'll not have another chance," said Ferdinand. "I'm not good for more than two days yet. Tell them to go out. I wish to see you alone. I wouldn't have sent for you, but, now that you're here, I might as well take advantage of it."

"Have you anything particular to say?" asked Knight, kindly.

"O, come," said Mason, with a smile which he meant to be good-natured, but which was only ghastly; "you're not going to be jealous of me at this time of day."

Knight looked at Miss Hofmann for permission, and then left the room with the nurse. But a minute had hardly elapsed before Miss Hofmann hurried into the adjoining apartment, with her face pale and discomposed.

"Go to him!" she exclaimed. "He's dying!"

When they reached him he was dead.

In the course of a few days his will was opened, and Knight came to the knowledge of his legacy. "He was a good, generous fellow," he said to Mrs. Mason and Miss Hofmann, "and I shall never be satisfied that he mightn't have recovered. It was a most extraordinary case." He was considerate enough of his audience to abstain from adding that he would give a great deal to have been able to make an autopsy. Miss Hofmann's wedding was, of course, not deferred. She was married in September, "very quietly." It seemed to her lover, in the interval, that she was very silent and thoughtful. But this was natural under the circumstances.